THE THREE DRUGS

And other selected stories

By

E. NESBIT

This edition published by Read Books Ltd.
Copyright © 2019 Read Books Ltd.
This book is copyright and may not be
reproduced or copied in any way without
the express permission of the publisher in writing

British Library Cataloguing-in-Publication Data
A catalogue record for this book is available
from the British Library

CONTENTS

E. Nesbit 5

THE THREE DRUGS 7

MAN-SIZE IN MARBLE 29

"JOHN CHARRINGTON'S WEDDING" 45

THE TWO PENNY SPELL 55

A COURSE IN MAGIC 65

E. Nesbit

Edith Nesbit was born in Kennington, Surrey in 1858. Her family moved around constantly during her youth, living variously in Brighton, Buckinghamshire, France, Spain and Germany, before settling for three years in Halstead in north-west Kent, a location which later inspired her well-known novel, *The Railway Children*. In 1880, Nesbit married Hubert Bland, and her writing talents – which had been in evidence during her teens – were quickly needed to bring in extra money.

Over the course of her life, Nesbit would go on to publish approximately 40 books for children, including novels, collections of stories and picture books. Among her best-known works are *The Story of the Treasure Seekers* (1898), *The Wouldbegoods* (1899) and *The Railway Children* (1906). Nesbit is regarded by many critics as the first truly 'modern' children's writer, in that she replaced the fantastical worlds utilised by authors such as Lewis Carroll with real-life settings marked by the occasional intrusion of magic. In this, Nesbit is seen as a precursor to writers such as J. K. Rowling and C. S. Lewis. Nesbit was also a lifelong socialist; in 1884 she was among the founding members of the influential Fabian Society. For much of her adult life she was an active lecturer and prolific writer on socialism.

Having suffered from lung cancer for some years, Nesbit died in 1924 at New Romney, Kent, aged 65.

THE THREE DRUGS

I

Roger Wroxham looked round his studio before he blew out the candle, and wondered whether, perhaps, he looked for the last time. It was large and empty, yet his trouble had filled it, and, pressing against him in the prison of those four walls, forced him out into the world, where lights and voices and the presence of other men should give him room to draw back, to set a space between it and him, to decide whether he would ever face it again—he and it alone together. The nature of his trouble is not germane to this story. There was a woman in it, of course, and money, and a friend, and regrets and embarrassments—and all of these reached out tendrils that wove and interwove till they made a puzzle-problem of which heart and brain were now weary. It was as though his life depended on his deciphering the straggling characters traced by some spider who, having fallen into the ink-well, had dragged clogged legs in a black zigzag across his map of the world.

He blew out the candle and went quietly downstairs. It was nine at night, a soft night of May in Paris. Where should he go? He thought of the Seine, and took—an omnibus. The chestnut trees of the Boulevards brushed against the sides of the one that he boarded blindly in the first light street. He did not know where the omnibus was going. It did not matter. When at last it stopped he got off, and so strange was the place to him that for an instant it almost seemed as though the trouble itself had been left behind. He did not feel it in the length of three or four streets that he traversed slowly. But in the open space, very light and lively, where he recognized the Taverne de Paris and knew himself in Montmartre, the trouble set its teeth in his heart again, and he broke away from the lamps and the talk to struggle with it in the dark quiet streets beyond.

A man braced for such a fight has little thought to spare for the detail of his surroundings. The next thing that Wroxham knew of the outside world was the fact that he had known for some time that he was not alone in the street. There was someone on the other side of the road keeping pace with him—yes, certainly keeping pace, for, as he slackened his own, the feet on the other pavement also went more slowly. And now they were four feet, not two. Where had the other man sprung from? He had not been there a moment ago. And now, from an archway a little ahead of him, a third man came.

Wroxham stopped. Then three men converged upon him, and, like a sudden magic-lantern picture on a sheet prepared, there came to him all that he had heard and read of Montmartre—dark archways, knives, Apaches, and men who went away from homes where they were beloved and never again returned. He, too—well, if he never returned again, it would be quicker than the Seine, and, in the event of ultramundane possibilities, safer.

He stood still and laughed in the face of the man who first reached him.

'Well, my friend?' said he, and at that the other two drew close.

'Monsieur walks late,' said the first, a little confused, as it seemed, by that laugh.

'And will walk still later, if it pleases him,' said Roger. 'Good night, my friends.'

'Ah!' said the second, 'friends do not say adieu so quickly. Monsieur will tell us the hour.'

'I have not a watch,' said Roger, quite truthfully.

'I will assist you to search for it,' said the third man, and laid a hand on his arm.

Roger threw it off. That was instinctive. One may be resigned to a man's knife between one's ribs, but not to his hands pawing one's shoulders. The man with the hand staggered back.

'The knife searches more surely,' said the second.

'No, no,' said the third quickly, 'he is too heavy. I for one will not carry him afterwards.'

They closed round him, hustling him between them. Their pale, degenerate faces spun and swung round him in the struggle. For there was a struggle. He had not meant that there should be a struggle. Someone would hear—someone would come.

But if any heard, none came. The street retained its empty silence, the houses, masked in close shutters, kept their reserve. The four were wrestling, all pressed together in a writhing bunch, drawing breath hardly through set teeth, their feet slipping, and not slipping, on the rounded cobble-stones.

The contact with these creatures, the smell of them, the warm, greasy texture of their flesh as, in the conflict, his face or neck met neck or face of theirs—Roger felt a cold rage possess him. He wrung two clammy hands apart and threw something off—something that staggered back clattering, fell in the gutter, and lay there.

It was then that Roger felt the knife. Its point glanced off the cigarette-case in his breast pocket and bit sharply at his inner arm. And at the sting of it Roger knew that he did not desire to die. He feigned a reeling weakness, relaxed his grip, swayed sideways, and then suddenly caught the other two in a new grip, crushed their faces together, flung them off, and ran. It was but for an instant that his feet were the only ones that echoed in the street. Then he knew that the others too were running.

It was like one of those nightmares wherein one runs for ever, leaden-footed, through a city of the dead. Roger turned sharply to the right. The sound of the other footsteps told that the pursuers also had turned that corner. Here was another street—a steep ascent. He ran more swiftly—he was running now for his life—the life that he held so cheap three minutes before. And all the streets were empty—empty like dream-streets, with all their windows dark and unhelpful, their doors fast closed against his need.

Far away down the street and across steep roofs lay Paris, poured out like a pool of light in the mist of the valley. But Roger was running with his head down—he saw nothing but the round heads of the cobble-stones. Only now and again he glanced to right or left, if perchance some window might show light to justify a cry for help, some door advance the welcome of an open inch.

There was at last such a door. He did not see it till it was almost behind him. Then there was the drag of the sudden stop—the eternal instant of indecision. Was there time? There must be. He dashed his fingers through the inch-crack, grazing the backs of them, leapt within, drew the door after him, felt madly for a lock or bolt, found a key, and, hanging his whole weight on it, strove to get the door home. The key turned. His left hand, by which he braced himself against the door-jamb, found a hook and pulled on it. Door and door-post met—the latch clicked—with a spring as it seemed. He turned the key, leaning against the door, which shook to the deep sobbing breaths that shook him, and to the panting bodies that pressed a moment without. Then someone cursed breathlessly outside; there was the sound of feet that went away.

Roger was alone in the strange darkness of an arched carriage-way, through the far end of which showed the fainter darkness of a court-yard, with black shapes of little formal tubbed orange trees. There was no sound at all there but the sound of his own desperate breathing; and, as he stood, the slow, warm blood crept down his wrist, to make a little pool in the hollow of his hanging, half-clenched hand. Suddenly he felt sick.

This house, of which he knew nothing, held for him no terrors. To him at that moment there were but three murderers in all the world, and where they were not, there safety was. But the spacious silence that soothed at first, presently clawed at the set, vibrating nerves already overstrained. He found himself listening, listening, and there was nothing to hear but the silence, and once, before he thought to twist his handkerchief round it, the drip of blood from his hand.

By and by, he knew that he was not alone in this house, for from far away there came the faint sound of a footstep, and, quite near, the faint answering echo of it. And at a window, high up on the other side of the courtyard, a light showed. Light and sound and echo intensified, the light passing window after window, till at last it moved across the courtyard, and the little trees threw back shifting shadows as it came towards him—a lamp in the hand of a man.

It was a short, bald man, with pointed beard and bright, friendly eyes. He held the lamp high as he came, and when he saw Roger, he drew his breath in an inspiration that spoke of surprise, sympathy, and pity.

'Hold! hold!' he said, in a singularly pleasant voice, 'there has been a misfortune? You are wounded, monsieur?'

'Apaches,' said Roger, and was surprised at the weakness of his own voice.

'Your hand?'

'My arm,' said Roger.

'Fortunately,' said the other, 'I am a surgeon. Allow me.'

He set the lamp on the step of a closed door, took off Roger's coat, and quickly tied his own handkerchief round the wounded arm.

'Now,' he said, 'courage! I am alone in the house. No one comes here but me. If you can walk up to my rooms, you will save us both much trouble. If you cannot, sit here and I will fetch you a cordial. But I advise you to try and walk. That *porte cochère* is, unfortunately, not very strong, and the lock is a common spring lock, and your friends may return with *their* friends; whereas the door across the courtyard is heavy and the bolts are new.'

Roger moved towards the heavy door whose bolts were new. The stairs seemed to go on for ever. The doctor lent his arm, but the carved banisters and their lively shadows whirled before Roger's eyes. Also, he seemed to be shod with lead, and to have in his legs bones that were red-hot. Then the stairs ceased, and there was light, and a cessation of the dragging of those leaden feet. He was on a couch, and his eyes might close. There was no need to move any more, nor to look, nor to listen.

When next he saw and heard, he was lying at ease, the close intimacy of a bandage clasping his arm, and in his mouth the vivid taste of some cordial.

The doctor was sitting in an armchair near a table, looking benevolent through gold-rimmed pince-nez.

'Better?' he said. 'No, lie still, you'll be a new man soon.'

'I am desolated,' said Roger, 'to have occasioned you all this trouble.'

'Not at all,' said the doctor. 'We live to heal, and it is a nasty cut, that in your arm. If you are wise, you will rest at present. I shall be honoured if you will be my guest for the night.'

Roger again murmured something about trouble.

'In a big house like this,' said the doctor, as it seemed a little sadly, 'there are many empty rooms, and some rooms which are not empty. There is a bed altogether at your service, monsieur, and I counsel you not to delay in seeking it. You can walk?'

Wroxham stood up. 'Why, yes,' he said, stretching himself. 'I feel, as you say, a new man.'

A narrow bed and rush-bottomed chair showed like doll's-house furniture in the large, high, gaunt room to which the doctor led him.

'You are too tired to undress yourself,' said the doctor, 'rest—only rest,' and covered him with a rug, roundly tucked him up, and left him.

'I leave the door open,' he said, 'in case you have any fever. Good night. Do not torment yourself. All goes well.'

Then he took away the lamp, and Wroxham lay on his back and saw the shadows of the window-frames cast on the wall by the moon now risen. His eyes, growing accustomed to the darkness, perceived the carving of the white-panelled walls and mantelpiece. There was a door in the room, another door from the one which the doctor had left open. Roger did not like open doors. The other door, however, was closed. He wondered where it led, and whether it were locked. Presently he got up to see. It was locked. He lay down again.

His arm gave him no pain, and the night's adventure did not seem to have overset his nerves. He felt, on the contrary, calm, confident, extraordinarily at ease, and master of himself. The trouble—how could that ever have seemed important? This calmness—it felt like the calmness that precedes sleep. Yet sleep was far from him. What was it that kept sleep away? The bed was comfortable—the pillows soft. What was it? It came to him presently that it was the scent which distracted him, worrying him with a memory that he could not define. A faint scent of—what was it? Perfumery? Yes—and camphor—and something else—something vaguely disquieting. He had not noticed it before he had risen and tried the handle of that other door. But now——. He covered his face with the sheet, but through the sheet he smelt it still. He rose and threw back one of the long french windows. It opened with a click and a jar, and he looked across the dark well of the courtyard. He leaned out, breathing the chill, pure air of the May night, but when he withdrew his head, the scent was there again. Camphor—perfume—and something else. What was it that it reminded him of? He had his knee on the bed-edge when the answer came to that question. It was the scent that had struck at him from a darkened room when, a child, clutching at a grown-up hand, he had been led to the bed where, amid flowers, something white lay under a sheet—his mother they had told him. It was the scent of death, disguised with drugs and perfumes.

He stood up and went, with carefully controlled swiftness, towards the open door. He wanted light and a human voice. The doctor was in the room upstairs; he——

The doctor was face to face with him on the landing, not a yard away, moving towards him quietly in shoeless feet.

'I can't sleep,' said Wroxham, a little wildly, 'it's too dark——'

'Come upstairs,' said the doctor, and Wroxham went.

There was comfort in the large, lighted room, with its shelves and shelves full of well-bound books, its tables heaped with papers and pamphlets—its air of natural everyday work. There was a warmth of red curtain at the windows. On the window ledge a plant in a pot, its leaves like red misshapen hearts. A green-shaded lamp stood on the table. A peaceful, pleasant interior.

'What's behind that door,' said Wroxham, abruptly—'that door downstairs?'

'Specimens,' the doctor answered, 'preserved specimens. My line is physiological research. You understand?'

So that was it.

'I feel quite well, you know,' said Wroxham, laboriously explaining—'fit as any man—only I can't sleep.'

'I see,' said the doctor.

'It's the scent from your specimens, I think,' Wroxham went on; 'there's something about that scent——'

'Yes,' said the doctor.

'It's very odd.' Wroxham was leaning his elbow on his knee and his chin on his hand. 'I feel so frightfully well—and yet——there's a strange feeling——'

'Yes,' said the doctor. 'Yes, tell me exactly what you feel.'

'I feel,' said Wroxham, slowly, 'like a man on the crest of a wave.'

The doctor stood up.

'You feel well, happy, full of life and energy—as though you could walk to the world's end, and yet——'

'And yet,' said Roger, 'as though my next step might be my last—as though I might step into my grave.'

He shuddered.

'Do you,' asked the doctor, anxiously—'do you feel thrills of pleasure—something like the first waves of chloroform—thrills running from your hair to your feet?'

'I felt all that,' said Roger, slowly, 'downstairs before I opened the window.'

The doctor looked at his watch, frowned and got up quickly. 'There is very little time,' he said.

Suddenly Roger felt an unexplained opposition stiffen his mind.

The doctor went to a long laboratory bench with bottle-filled shelves above it, and on it crucibles and retorts, test-tubes, beakers—all a chemist's apparatus—reached a bottle from a shelf, and measured out certain drops into a graduated glass, added water, and stirred it with a glass rod.

'Drink that,' he said.

'No,' said Roger, and as he spoke a thrill like the first thrill of the first chloroform wave swept through him, and it was a thrill, not of pleasure, but of pain. 'No,' he said, and 'Ah!' for the pain was sharp.

'If you don't drink,' said the doctor, carefully, 'you are a dead man.'

'You may be giving me poison,' Roger gasped, his hands at his heart.

'I may,' said the doctor. 'What do you suppose poison makes you feel like? What do you feel like now?'

'I feel,' said Roger, 'like death.'

Every nerve, every muscle thrilled to a pain not too intense to be underlined by a shuddering nausea.

'Then drink,' cried the doctor, in tones of such cordial entreaty, such evident anxiety, that Wroxham half held his hand out for the glass. 'Drink! Believe me, it is your only chance.'

Again the pain swept through him like an electric current. The beads of sweat sprang out on his forehead.

'That wound,' the doctor pleaded, standing over him with the glass held out. 'For God's sake, drink! Don't you understand, man? You *are* poisoned. Your wound——'

'The knife?' Wroxham murmured, and as he spoke, his eyes seemed to swell in his head, and his head itself to grow enormous. 'Do you know the poison—and its antidote?'

'I know all.' The doctor soothed him. 'Drink, then, my friend.'

As the pain caught him again in a clasp more close than any lover's he clutched at the glass and drank. The drug met the pain and mastered it. Roger, in the ecstasy of pain's cessation, saw the world fade and go out in a haze of vivid violet.

Faint films of lassitude, shot with contentment, wrapped him round. He lay passive, as a man lies in the convalescence that follows a long fight with Death. Fold on fold of white peace lay all about him.

'I'm better now,' he said, in a voice that was a whisper—tried to raise his hand from where it lay helpless in his sight, failed, and lay looking at it in confident repose—'much better.'

'Yes,' said the doctor, and his pleasant, soft voice had grown softer, pleasanter. 'You are now in the second stage. An interval is necessary before you can pass to the third. I will enliven the interval by conversation. Is there anything you would like to know?'

'Nothing,' said Roger; 'I am quite contented.'

'This is very interesting,' said the doctor. 'Tell me exactly how you feel.'

Roger faintly and slowly told him.

'Ah!' the doctor said, 'I have not before heard this. You are the only one of them all who ever passed the first stage. The others——'

'The others?' said Roger, but he did not care much about the others.

'The others,' said the doctor frowning, 'were unsound. Decadent students, degenerate, Apaches. You are highly trained—in fine physical condition. And your brain! God be good to the Apaches, who so delicately excited it to just the degree of activity needed for my purpose.'

'The others?' Wroxham insisted.

'The others? They are in the room whose door was locked. Look—you should be able to see them. The second drug should lay your consciousness before me, like a sheet of white paper on which I can write what I choose. If I choose that you should see my specimens—*Allons donc*. I have no secrets from you now. Look—look—strain your eyes. In theory, I know all that you can do and feel and see in this second stage. But practically—enlighten me—look—shut your eyes and look!'

Roger closed his eyes and looked. He saw the gaunt, uncarpeted staircase, the open doors of the big rooms, passed to the locked door, and it opened at his touch. The room inside was like the others, spacious and panelled. A lighted lamp with a blue shade hung from the ceiling, and below it an effect of spread whiteness. Roger looked. There *were* things to be seen.

With a shudder he opened his eyes on the doctor's delightful room, the doctor's intent face.

'What did you see?' the doctor asked. 'Tell me!'

'Did you kill them all?' Roger asked back.

'They died—of their own inherent weakness,' the doctor said. 'And you saw them?'

'I saw,' said Roger, 'the quiet people lying all along the floor in their death clothes—the people who have come in at that door of yours that is a trap—for robbery, or curiosity, or shelter, and never gone out any more.'

'Right,' said the doctor. 'Right. My theory is proved at every point. You can see what I choose you to see. Yes, decadents all. It was in embalming that I was a specialist before I began these other investigations.'

'What,' Roger whispered—'what is it all for?'

'To make the superman,' said the doctor. 'I will tell you.'

He told. It was a long story—the story of a man's life, a man's work, a man's dreams, hopes, ambitions.

'The secret of life,' the doctor ended. 'That is what all the alchemists sought. They sought it where Fate pleased. I sought it where I have found it—in death.'

Roger thought of the room behind the locked door.

'And the secret is?' he asked.

'I have told you,' said the doctor impatiently; 'it is in the third drug that life—splendid, superhuman life—is found. I have tried it on animals. Always they became perfect, all that an animal should be. And more, too—much more. They were too perfect, too near humanity. They looked at me with human eyes. I could not let them live. Such animals it is not necessary to embalm. I had a laboratory in those days—and assistants. They called me the Prince of Vivisectors.'

The man on the sofa shuddered.

'I am naturally,' the doctor went on, 'a tender-hearted man. You see it in my face; my voice proclaims it. Think what I have suffered in the sufferings of these poor beasts who never injured me. My God! Bear witness that I have not buried my talent. I have been faithful. I have laid down all—love, and joy, and pity, and the little beautiful things of life—all, all, on the altar of science, and seen them consume away. I deserve my heaven, if ever man did. And now by all the saints in heaven I am near it!'

'What is the third drug?' Roger asked, lying limp and flat on his couch.

'It is the Elixir of Life,' said the doctor. 'I am not its discoverer; the old alchemists knew it well, but they failed because they sought to apply the elixir to a normal—that is, a diseased and faulty—body. I knew better. One must have first a body abnormally healthy, abnormally strong. Then, not the elixir, but the two drugs that prepare. The first excites prematurely the natural conflict between the principles of life and death, and then, just at the point where Death is about to win his victory, the second drug intensifies life so that it conquers—intensifies, and yet chastens. Then the whole life of the subject, risen to an ecstasy, falls prone in an almost voluntary submission to the coming super-life. Submission—submission! The garrison must surrender before the splendid conqueror can enter and make the citadel his own. Do you understand? Do you submit?'

'I submit,' said Roger, for, indeed, he did. 'But—soon—quite soon —I will not submit.'

He was too weak to be wise, or those words had remained unspoken.

The doctor sprang to his feet.

'It works too quickly!' he cried. 'Everything works too quickly with you. Your condition is too perfect. So now I bind you.'

From a drawer beneath the bench where the bottles gleamed, the doctor drew rolls of bandages—violet, like the haze that had drowned, at the urgence of the second drug, the consciousness of Roger. He moved, faintly resistant, on his couch. The doctor's hands, most gently, most irresistibly, controlled his movement.

'Lie still,' said the gentle, charming voice. 'Lie still; all is well.' The clever, soft hands were unrolling the bandages—passing them round arms and throat—under and over the soft narrow couch. 'I cannot risk your life, my poor boy. The least movement of yours might ruin everything. The third drug, like the first, must be offered directly to the blood which absorbs it. I bound the first drug as an unguent upon your knife-wound.'

The swift hands, the soft bandages, passed back and forth, over and under—flashes of violet passed to and fro in the air, like the shuttle of a weaver through his warp. As the bandage clasped his knees, Roger moved.

'For God's sake, no!' the doctor cried; 'the time is so near. If you cease to submit it is death.'

With an incredible, accelerated swiftness he swept the bandages round and round knees and ankles, drew a deep breath—stood upright.

'I must make an incision,' he said—'in the head this time. It will not hurt. See! I spray it with the Constantia Nepenthe; that also I discovered. My boy, in a moment you know all things—you are as God. For God's sake, be patient. Preserve your submission.'

And Roger, with life and will resurgent hammering at his heart, preserved it.

He did not feel the knife that made the cross-cut on his temple, but he felt the hot spurt of blood that followed the cut; he felt the cool flap of a plaster, spread with some sweet, clean-smelling unguent that met the blood and stanched it. There was a moment—or was it hours?—of nothingness. Then from that cut on his forehead there seemed to radiate threads of infinite length, and of a strength that one could trust to—threads that linked one to all knowledge past and present. He felt that he controlled all wisdom, as a driver controls his four-in-hand. Knowledge, he perceived, belonged to him, as the air belongs to the eagle. He swam in it, as a great fish in a limitless ocean.

He opened his eyes and met those of the doctor, who sighed as one to whom breath has grown difficult.

'Ah, all goes well. Oh, my boy, was it not worth it? What do you feel?'

'I. Know. Everything,' said Roger, with full stops between the words.

'Everything? The future?'

'No. I know all that man has ever known.'

'Look back—into the past. See someone. See Pharaoh. You see him—on his throne?'

'Not on his throne. He is whispering in a corner of his great gardens to a girl, who is the daughter of a water-carrier.'

'Bah! Any poet of my dozen decadents, who lie so still could have told me that. Tell me secrets—the *Masque de Fer*.'

The other told a tale, wild and incredible, but it satisfied the teller.

'That too—it might be imagination. Tell me the name of the woman I loved and——'

The echo of the name of the anaesthetic came to Roger; 'Constantia,' said he, in an even voice.

'Ah,' the doctor cried, 'now I see you know all things. It was not murder. I hoped to dower her with all the splendours of the superlife.'

'Her bones lie under the lilacs, where you used to kiss her in the spring,' said Roger, quite without knowing what it was that he was going to say.

'It is enough,' the doctor cried. He sprang up, ranged certain bottles and glasses on a table convenient to his chair. 'You know all things. It was not a dream, this, the dream of my life. It is true. It is a fact accomplished. Now I, too, will know all things. I will be as the gods.'

He sought among leather cases on a far table, and came back swiftly into the circle of light that lay below the green-shaded lamp.

Roger, floating contentedly on the new sea of knowledge that seemed to support him, turned eyes on the trouble that had driven him out of that large, empty studio so long ago, so far away. His new-found wisdom laughed at that problem, laughed and solved it. 'To end that trouble I must do so-and-so, say such-and-such,' Roger told himself again and again.

And now the doctor, standing by the table, laid on it his pale, plump hand outspread. He drew a knife from a case—a long, shiny knife—and scored his hand across and across its back, as a cook scores pork for cooking. The slow blood followed the cuts in beads and lines.

Into the cuts he dropped a green liquid from a little bottle, replaced its stopper, bound up his hand and sat down.

'The beginning of the first stage,' he said; 'almost at once I shall begin to be a new man. It will work quickly. My body, like yours, is sane and healthy.'

There was a long silence.

'Oh, but this is good,' the doctor broke it to say. 'I feel the hand of Life sweeping my nerves like harp-strings.'

Roger had been thinking, the old common sense that guides an ordinary man breaking through this consciousness of illimitable wisdom. 'You had better,' he said, 'unbind me; when the hand of Death sweeps your nerves, you may need help.'

'No,' the doctor said, 'and no, and no, and no many times. I am afraid of you. You know all things, and even in your body you are stronger than I. When I, too, am a god, and filled with the wine of knowledge, I will loose you, and together we will drink of the fourth drug—the mordant that shall fix the others and set us eternally on a level with the immortals.'

'Just as you like, of course,' said Roger, with a conscious effort after commonplace. Then suddenly, not commonplace any more—

'Loose me!' he cried; 'loose me, I tell you! I am wiser than you.'

'You are also stronger,' said the doctor, and then suddenly and irresistibly the pain caught him. Roger saw his face contorted with agony, his hands clench on the arm of his chair; and it seemed that, either this man was less able to bear pain than he, or that the pain was much more violent than had been his own. Between the grippings of the anguish the doctor dragged on his watch-chain; the watch leapt from his pocket, and rattled as his trembling hand laid it on the table.

'Not yet,' he said, when he had looked at its face, 'not yet, not yet, not yet.' It seemed to Roger, lying there bound, that the other man repeated those words for long days and weeks. And the plump, pale hand, writhing and distorted by anguish, again and again drew near to take the glass that stood ready on the table, and with convulsive self-restraint again and again drew back without it.

The short May night was waning—the shiver of dawn rustled the leaves of the plant whose leaves were like red misshaped hearts.

'Now!' The doctor screamed the word, grasped the glass, drained it and sank back in his chair. His hand struck the table beside him.

Looking at his limp body and head thrown back, one could almost see the cessation of pain, the coming of kind oblivion.

III

The dawn had grown to daylight, a poor, grey, rain-stained daylight, not strong enough to pierce the curtains and persiennes, and yet not so weak but that it could mock the lamp, now burnt low and smelling vilely.

Roger lay very still on his couch, a man wounded, anxious, and extravagantly tired. In those hours of long, slow dawning, face to face with the unconscious figure in the chair, he had felt, slowly and little by little, the recession of that sea of knowledge on which he had felt himself float in such content. The sea had withdrawn itself, leaving him high and dry on the shore of the normal. The only relic that he had clung to and that he still grasped was the answer to the problem of the trouble—the only wisdom that he had put into words. These words remained to him, and he knew that they held wisdom—very simple wisdom, too.

'To end the trouble, I must do so-and-so and say such-and-such.'

But of all that had seemed to set him on a pinnacle, had evened him with the immortals, nothing else was left. He was just Roger Wroxham—wounded, and bound, in a locked house, one of whose rooms was full of very quiet people, and in another room himself and a dead man. For now it was so long since the doctor had moved that it seemed he must be dead. He had got to know every line of that room, every fold of drapery, every flower on the wall-paper, the number of the books, the shapes and sizes of things. Now he could no longer look at these. He looked at the other man.

Slowly a dampness spread itself over Wroxham's forehead and tingled among the roots of his hair. He writhed in his bonds. They held fast. He could not move hand or foot. Only his head could turn a little, so that he could at will see the doctor or not see him. A shaft of desolate light pierced the persienne at its hinge and rested on the table, where an overturned glass lay.

Wroxham thrilled from head to foot. The body in the chair stirred—hardly stirred—shivered rather—and a very faint, far-away voice said:

'Now the third—give me the third.'

'What?' said Roger, stupidly; and he had to clear his throat twice before he could say even that.

'The moment is now,' said the doctor. 'I remember all. I made you a god. Give me the third drug.'

'Where is it?' Roger asked.

'It is at my elbow,' the doctor murmured. 'I submit—I submit. Give me the third drug, and let me be as you are.'

'As *I* am?' said Roger. 'You forget. *I* am bound.'

'Break your bonds,' the doctor urged, in a quick, small voice. 'I trust you now. You are stronger than all men, as you are wiser. Stretch your muscles, and the bandages will fall asunder like snow-wreaths.'

'It is too late,' Wroxham said, and laughed; 'all that is over. I am not wise any more, and I have only the strength of a man. I am tired and wounded. I cannot break your bonds—I cannot help you!'

'But if you cannot help me—it is death,' said the doctor.

'It is death,' said Roger. 'Do you feel it coming on you?'

'I feel life returning,' said the doctor; 'it is now the moment—the one possible moment. And I cannot reach it. Oh, give it me—give it me!'

Then Roger cried out suddenly, in a loud voice: 'Now, by God in heaven, you damned decadent, I am *glad* that I cannot give it. Yes if it costs me my life, it's worth it, you madman, so that your life ends too. Now be silent, and die like a man, if you have it in you.'

Only one word seemed to reach the man in the chair.

'A decadent!' he repeated. 'I? But no, I am like you—I see what I will. I close my eyes, and I see—no—not that—ah!—not that!' He writhed faintly in his chair, and to Roger it seemed that for that writhing figure there would be no return of power and life and will.

'Not that,' he moaned. 'Not that,' and writhed in a gasping anguish that bore no more words.

Roger lay and watched him, and presently he writhed from the chair to the floor, tearing feebly at it with his fingers, moaned, shuddered, and lay very still.

Of all that befell Roger in that house, the worst was now. For now he knew that he was alone with the dead, and between him and death stretched certain hours and days. For the *porte cochère* was locked; the doors of the house itself were locked—heavy doors and locks new.

'I am alone in the house,' the doctor had said. 'No one comes here but me.'

No one would come. He would die there—he, Roger Wroxham—'poor old Roger Wroxham, who was no one's enemy but his own.' Tears pricked his eyes. He shook his head impatiently and they fell from his lashes.

'You fool,' he said, 'can't *you* die like a man either?'

Then he set his teeth and made himself lie still. It seemed to him that now Despair laid her hand on his heart. But, to speak truth, it was Hope whose hand lay there. This was so much more than a man should be called on to bear—it could not be true. It was an evil dream. He would wake presently. Or if it were, indeed, real—then someone would come, someone must come. God could not let nobody come to save him.

And late at night, when heart and brain had been stretched to the point where both break and let in the sea of madness, someone came.

The interminable day had worn itself out. Roger had screamed, yelled, shouted till his throat was dried up, his lips baked and cracked. No one heard. How should they? The twilight had thickened and thickened, till at last it made a shroud for the dead man on the floor by the chair. And there were other dead men in that house; and as Roger ceased to see the one he saw the others—the quiet, awful faces the lean hands, the straight, stiff limbs laid out one beyond another in the room of death. They at least were not bound. If they should rise in their white wrappings and, crossing that empty sleeping chamber very softly, come slowly up the stairs—

A stair creaked.

His ears, strained with hours of listening, thought themselves befooled. But his cowering heart knew better.

Again a stair creaked. There was a hand on the door.

'Then it is all over,' said Roger in the darkness, 'and I *am* mad.'

The door opened very slowly, very cautiously. There was no light. Only the sound of soft feet and draperies that rustled.

Then suddenly a match spurted—light struck at his eyes; a flicker of lit candle-wick steadying to flame. And the things that had come were not those quiet people creeping up to match their death with his death in life, but human creatures, alive, breathing, with eyes that moved and glittered, lips that breathed and spoke.

'He must be here,' one said. 'Lisette watched all day; he never came out. He must be here—there is nowhere else.'

Then they set up the candle-end on the table, and he saw their faces. They were the Apaches who had set on him in that lonely street, and who had sought him here—to set on him again.

He sucked his dry tongue, licked his dry lips, and cried aloud:

'Here I am! Oh, kill me! For the love of God, brothers, kill me *now*!'

And even before he spoke, they had seen him, and seen what lay on the floor.

'He died this morning. I am bound. Kill me, brothers; I cannot die slowly here alone. Oh, kill me, for Christ's sake!'

But already the three were pressing on each other at a doorway suddenly grown too narrow. They could kill a living man, but they could not face death, quiet, enthroned.

'For the love of Christ,' Roger screamed, 'have pity! Kill me outright! Come back—come back!'

And then, since even Apaches are human, one of them did come back. It was the one he had flung into the gutter. The feet of the others sounded on the stairs as he caught up the candle and bent over Roger, knife in hand.

'Make sure,' said Roger, through set teeth.

'*Nom d'un nom*,' said the Apache, with worse words, and cut the bandages here, and here, and here again, and there, and lower, to the very feet.

Then this good Samaritan helped Roger to rise, and when he could not stand, the Samaritan half pulled, half carried him down those many steps, till they came upon the others putting on their boots at the stair-foot.

Then between them the three men who could walk carried the other out and slammed the outer door, and presently set him against a gate-post in another street, and went their wicked ways.

And after a time, a girl with furtive eyes brought brandy and hoarse, muttered kindnesses, and slid away in the shadows.

Against that gate-post the police came upon him. They took him to the address they found on him. When they came to question him he said, 'Apaches', and his late variations on that theme were deemed sufficient, though not one of them touched truth or spoke of the third drug.

There has never been anything in the papers about that house. I think it is still closed, and inside it still lie in the locked room the very quiet people; and above, there is the room with the narrow couch and the scattered, cut, violet bandages, and the thing on the floor by the chair, under the lamp that burned itself out in that May dawning.

MAN-SIZE IN MARBLE

Although every word of this story is as true as despair, I do not expect people to believe it. Nowadays a "rational explanation" is required before belief is possible. Let me then, at once, offer the "rational explanation" which finds most favour among those who have heard the tale of my life's tragedy. It is held that we were "under a delusion," Laura and I, on that 31st of October; and that this supposition places the whole matter on a satisfactory and believable basis. The reader can judge, when he, too, has heard my story, how far this is an "explanation," and in what sense it is "rational." There were three who took part in this: Laura and I and another man. The other man still lives, and can speak to the truth of the least credible part of my story.

I never in my life knew what it was to have as much money as I required to supply the most ordinary needs--good colours, books, and cab-fares--and when we were married we knew quite well that we should only be able to live at all by "strict punctuality and attention to business." I used to paint in those days, and Laura used to write, and we felt sure we could keep the pot at least simmering. Living in town was out of the question, so we went to look for a cottage in the country, which should be at once sanitary and picturesque. So rarely do these two qualities meet in one cottage that our search was for some time quite fruitless. We tried advertisements, but most of the desirable rural residences which we did look at proved to be lacking in both essentials, and when a cottage chanced to have drains it always had stucco as well and was shaped like a tea-caddy. And if we found a vine or rose-covered porch, corruption invariably lurked within. Our minds got so befogged by the eloquence of house-agents and the rival disadvantages of the fever-traps and outrages to beauty which we had seen and scorned, that I very much doubt whether either of us, on our wedding morning, knew the difference between a house and a haystack. But when we got away from friends and house-agents, on our honeymoon, our wits grew clear again, and we knew a pretty cottage when at last we saw one. It was at Brenzett--a little village set on a hill over against the southern marshes. We had gone there, from the seaside village where we were staying, to see the church, and two fields from the church we found this cottage. It stood quite by itself, about two miles from the village. It was a long, low building, with rooms sticking out in unexpected places. There was a bit of stone-work--ivy-covered and moss-grown, just two old rooms, all that was left of a big house that had once stood there--and round this stone-work the house had grown up. Stripped of its roses and jasmine it would have been hideous. As it stood it was charming, and after a brief examination we took it. It was absurdly cheap. The rest of our honeymoon we spent in grubbing about in second-hand shops in the county town, picking up bits of old oak and Chippendale chairs for our furnishing. We wound up with a run up to town and a visit to Liberty's, and soon the low oak-beamed lattice-windowed rooms began to be home. There was a jolly old-fashioned garden, with grass paths, and no end of hollyhocks and sunflowers, and big lilies. From the window you could see the marsh-pastures, and beyond them the blue, thin line of the sea. We were as happy as the summer was glorious, and settled down into work sooner than we ourselves expected. I was never tired of sketching the view and the wonderful cloud effects from the open lattice, and Laura would sit at the table and write verses about them, in which I mostly played the part of foreground.

We got a tall old peasant woman to do for us. Her face and figure were good, though her cooking was of the homeliest; but she understood all about gardening, and told us all the old names of the coppices and cornfields, and the stories of the smugglers and highwaymen, and, better still, of the "things that walked," and of the "sights" which met one in lonely glens of a starlight night. She was a great comfort to us, because Laura hated housekeeping as much as I loved folklore, and we soon came to leave all the domestic business to Mrs. Dorman, and to use her legends in little magazine stories which brought in the jingling guinea.

We had three months of married happiness, and did not have a single quarrel. One October evening I had been down to smoke a pipe with the doctor--our only neighbour--a pleasant young Irishman. Laura had stayed at home to finish a comic sketch of a village episode for the Monthly Marplot. I left her laughing over her own jokes, and came in to find her a crumpled heap of pale muslin weeping on the window seat.

"Good heavens, my darling, what's the matter?" I cried, taking her in my arms. She leaned her little dark head against my shoulder and went on crying. I had never seen her cry before--we had always been so happy, you see--and I felt sure some frightful misfortune had happened.

"What is the matter? Do speak."

"It's Mrs. Dorman," she sobbed.

"What has she done?" I inquired, immensely relieved.

"She says she must go before the end of the month, and she says her niece is ill; she's gone down to see her now, but I don't believe that's the reason, because her niece is always ill. I believe someone has been setting her against us. Her manner was so queer---"

"Never mind, Pussy," I said; "whatever you do, don't cry, or I shall have to cry too, to keep you in countenance, and then you'll never respect your man again!"

She dried her eyes obediently on my handkerchief, and even smiled faintly.

"But you see," she went on, "it is really serious, because these village people are so sheepy, and if one won't do a thing you may be quite sure none of the others will. And I shall have to cook the dinners, and wash up the hateful greasy plates; and you'll have to carry cans of water about, and clean the boots and knives--and we shall never have any time for work, or earn any money, or anything. We shall have to work all day, and only be able to rest when we are waiting for the kettle to boil!"

I represented to her that even if we had to perform these duties, the day would still present some margin for other toils and recreations. But she refused to see the matter in any but the greyest light. She was very unreasonable, my Laura, but I could not have loved her any more if she had been as reasonable as Whately.

"I'll speak to Mrs. Dorman when she comes back, and see if I can't come to terms with her," I said. "Perhaps she wants a rise in her screw. It will be all right. Let's walk up to the church."

The church was a large and lonely one, and we loved to go there, especially upon bright nights. The path skirted a wood, cut through it once, and ran along the crest of the hill through two meadows, and round the churchyard wall, over which the old yews loomed in black masses of shadow. This path, which was partly paved, was called "the bier-balk," for it had long been the way by which the corpses had been carried to burial. The churchyard was richly treed, and was shaded by great elms which stood just outside and stretched their majestic arms in benediction over the happy dead. A large, low porch let one into the building by a Norman doorway and a heavy oak door studded with iron. Inside, the arches rose into darkness, and between them the reticulated windows, which stood out white in the moonlight. In the chancel, the windows were of rich glass, which showed in faint light their noble colouring, and made the black oak of the choir pews hardly more solid than the shadows. But on each side of the altar lay a grey marble figure of a knight in full plate armour lying upon a low slab, with hands held up in everlasting prayer, and these figures, oddly enough, were always to be seen if there was any glimmer of light in the church. Their names were lost, but the peasants told of them that they had been fierce and wicked men, marauders by land and sea, who had been the scourge of their time, and had been guilty of deeds so foul that the house they had lived in--the big house, by the way, that had stood on the site of our cottage--had been stricken by lightning and the vengeance of Heaven. But for all that, the gold of their heirs had bought them a place in the church. Looking at the bad hard faces reproduced in the marble, this story was easily believed.

The church looked at its best and weirdest on that night, for the shadows of the yew trees fell through the windows upon the floor of the nave and touched the pillars with tattered shade. We sat down together without speaking, and watched the solemn beauty of the old church, with some of that awe which inspired its early builders. We walked to the chancel and looked at the sleeping warriors. Then we rested some time on the stone seat in the porch, looking out over the stretch of quiet moonlit meadows, feeling in every fibre of our being the peace of the night and of our happy love; and came away at last with a sense that even scrubbing and blackleading were but small troubles at their worst.

Mrs. Dorman had come back from the village, and I at once invited her to a tête-à-tête.

"Now, Mrs. Dorman," I said, when I had got her into my painting room, "what's all this about your not staying with us?"

"I should be glad to get away, sir, before the end of the month," she answered, with her usual placid dignity.

"Have you any fault to find, Mrs. Dorman?"

"None at all, sir; you and your lady have always been most kind, I'm sure---"

"Well, what is it? Are your wages not high enough?"

"No, sir, I gets quite enough."

"Then why not stay?"

"I'd rather not"--with some hesitation--"my niece is ill."

"But your niece has been ill ever since we came."

No answer. There was a long and awkward silence. I broke it.

"Can't you stay for another month?" I asked.

"No, sir. I'm bound to go by Thursday."

And this was Monday!

"Well, I must say, I think you might have let us know before. There's no time now to get any one else, and your mistress is not fit to do heavy housework. Can't you stay till next week?"

"I might be able to come back next week."

I was now convinced that all she wanted was a brief holiday, which we should have been willing enough to let her have, as soon as we could get a substitute.

"But why must you go this week?" I persisted. "Come, out with it."

Mrs. Dorman drew the little shawl, which she always wore, tightly across her bosom, as though she were cold. Then she said, with a sort of effort---

"They say, sir, as this was a big house in Catholic times, and there was a many deeds done here."

The nature of the "deeds" might be vaguely inferred from the inflection of Mrs. Dorman's voice--which was enough to make one's blood run cold. I was glad that Laura was not in the room. She was always nervous, as highly-strung natures are, and I felt that these tales about our house, told by this old peasant woman, with her impressive manner and contagious credulity, might have made our home less dear to my wife.

"Tell me all about it, Mrs. Dorman," I said; "you needn't mind about telling me. I'm not like the young people who make fun of such things."

Which was partly true.

"Well, sir"--she sank her voice--"you may have seen in the church, beside the altar, two shapes."

"You mean the effigies of the knights in armour," I said cheerfully.

"I mean them two bodies, drawed out man-size in marble," she returned, and I had to admit that her description was a thousand times more graphic than mine, to say nothing of a certain weird force and uncanniness about the phrase "drawed out man-size in marble."

"They do say, as on All Saints' Eve them two bodies sits up on their slabs, and gets off of them, and then walks down the aisle, in their marble"--(another good phrase, Mrs. Dorman)--"and as the church clock strikes eleven they walks out of the church door, and over the graves, and along the bier-balk, and if it's a wet night there's the marks of their feet in the morning."

"And where do they go?" I asked, rather fascinated.

"They comes back here to their home, sir, and if any one meets them---"

"Well, what then?" I asked.

But no--not another word could I get from her, save that her niece was ill and she must go. After what I had heard I scorned to discuss the niece, and tried to get from Mrs. Dorman more details of the legend. I could get nothing but warnings.

"Whatever you do, sir, lock the door early on All Saints' Eve, and make the cross-sign over the doorstep and on the windows."

"But has any one ever seen these things?" I persisted.

"That's not for me to say. I know what I know, sir."

"Well, who was here last year?"

"No one, sir; the lady as owned the house only stayed here in summer, and she always went to London a full month afore the night. And I'm sorry to inconvenience you and your lady, but my niece is ill and I must go on Thursday."

I could have shaken her for her absurd reiteration of that obvious fiction, after she had told me her real reasons.

She was determined to go, nor could our united entreaties move her in the least.

I did not tell Laura the legend of the shapes that "walked in their marble," partly because a legend concerning our house might perhaps trouble my wife, and partly, I think, from some more occult reason. This was not quite the same to me as any other story, and I did not want to talk about it till the day was over. I had very soon ceased to think of the legend, however. I was painting a portrait of Laura, against the lattice window, and I could not think of much else. I had got a splendid background of yellow and grey sunset, and was working away with enthusiasm at her lace. On Thursday Mrs. Dorman went. She relented, at parting, so far as to say---

"Don't you put yourself about too much, ma'am, and if there's any little thing I can do next week, I'm sure I shan't mind."

From which I inferred that she wished to come back to us after Hallowe'en. Up to the last she adhered to the fiction of the niece with touching fidelity.

Thursday passed off pretty well. Laura showed marked ability in the matter of steak and potatoes, and I confess that my knives, and the plates, which I insisted upon washing, were better done than I had dared to expect.

Friday came. It is about what happened on that Friday that this is written. I wonder if I should have believed it, if any one had told it to me. I will write the story of it as quickly and plainly as I can. Everything that happened on that day is burnt into my brain. I shall not forget anything, nor leave anything out.

I got up early, I remember, and lighted the kitchen fire, and had just achieved a smoky success, when my little wife came running down, as sunny and sweet as the clear October morning itself. We prepared breakfast together, and found it very good fun. The housework was soon done, and when brushes and brooms and pails were quiet again, the house was still indeed. It is wonderful what a difference one makes in a house. We really missed Mrs. Dorman, quite apart from considerations concerning pots and pans. We spent the day in dusting our books and putting them straight, and dined gaily on cold steak and coffee. Laura was, if possible, brighter and gayer and sweeter than usual, and I began to think that a little domestic toil was really good for her. We had never been so merry since we were married, and the walk we had that afternoon was, I think, the happiest time of all my life. When we had watched the deep scarlet clouds slowly pale into leaden grey against a pale-green sky, and saw the white mists curl up along the hedgerows in the distant marsh, we came back to the house, silently, hand in hand.

"You are sad, my darling," I said, half-jestingly, as we sat down together in our little parlour. I expected a disclaimer, for my own silence had been the silence of complete happiness. To my surprise she said---

"Yes. I think I am sad, or rather I am uneasy. I don't think I'm very well. I have shivered three or four times since we came in, and it is not cold, is it?"

"No," I said, and hoped it was not a chill caught from the treacherous mists that roll up from the marshes in the dying light. No--she said, she did not think so. Then, after a silence, she spoke suddenly---

"Do you ever have presentiments of evil?"

"No," I said, smiling, "and I shouldn't believe in them if I had."

"I do," she went on; "the night my father died I knew it, though he was right away in the north of Scotland." I did not answer in words.

She sat looking at the fire for some time in silence, gently stroking my hand. At last she sprang up, came behind me, and, drawing my head back, kissed me.

"There, it's over now," she said. "What a baby I am! Come, light the candles, and we'll have some of these new Rubinstein duets."

And we spent a happy hour or two at the piano.

At about half-past ten I began to long for the good-night pipe, but Laura looked so white that I felt it would be brutal of me to fill our sitting-room with the fumes of strong cavendish.

"I'll take my pipe outside," I said.

"Let me come, too."

"No, sweetheart, not to-night; you're much too tired. I shan't be long. Get to bed, or I shall have an invalid to nurse to-morrow as well as the boots to clean."

I kissed her and was turning to go, when she flung her arms round my neck, and held me as if she would never let me go again. I stroked her hair.

"Come, Pussy, you're over-tired. The housework has been too much for you."

She loosened her clasp a little and drew a deep breath.

"No. We've been very happy to-day, Jack, haven't we? Don't stay out too long."

"I won't, my dearie."

I strolled out of the front door, leaving it unlatched. What a night it was! The jagged masses of heavy dark cloud were rolling at intervals from horizon to horizon, and thin white wreaths covered the stars. Through all the rush of the cloud river, the moon swam, breasting the waves and disappearing again in the darkness. When now and again her light reached the woodlands they seemed to be slowly and noiselessly waving in time to the swing of the clouds above them. There was a strange grey light over all the earth; the fields had that shadowy bloom over them which only comes from the marriage of dew and moonshine, or frost and starlight.

I walked up and down, drinking in the beauty of the quiet earth and the changing sky. The night was absolutely silent. Nothing seemed to be abroad. There was no skurrying of rabbits, or twitter of the half-asleep birds. And though the clouds went sailing across the sky, the wind that drove them never came low enough to rustle the dead leaves in the woodland paths. Across the meadows I could see the church tower standing out black and grey against the sky. I walked there thinking over our three months of happiness--and of my wife, her dear eyes, her loving ways. Oh, my little girl! my own little girl; what a vision came then of a long, glad life for you and me together!

I heard a bell-beat from the church. Eleven already! I turned to go in, but the night held me. I could not go back into our little warm rooms yet. I would go up to the church. I felt vaguely that it would be good to carry my love and thankfulness to the sanctuary whither so many loads of sorrow and gladness had been borne by the men and women of the dead years.

I looked in at the low window as I went by. Laura was half lying on her chair in front of the fire. I could not see her face, only her little head showed dark against the pale blue wall. She was quite still. Asleep, no doubt. My heart reached out to her, as

I went on. There must be a God, I thought, and a God who was good. How otherwise could anything so sweet and dear as she have ever been imagined?

I walked slowly along the edge of the wood. A sound broke the stillness of the night, it was a rustling in the wood. I stopped and listened. The sound stopped too. I went on, and now distinctly heard another step than mine answer mine like an echo. It was a poacher or a wood-stealer, most likely, for these were not unknown in our Arcadian neighbourhood. But whoever it was, he was a fool not to step more lightly. I turned into the wood, and now the footstep seemed to come from the path I had just left. It must be an echo, I thought. The wood looked perfect in the moonlight. The large dying ferns and the brushwood showed where through thinning foliage the pale light came down. The tree trunks stood up like Gothic columns all around me. They reminded me of the church, and I turned into the bier-balk, and passed through the corpse-gate between the graves to the low porch. I paused for a moment on the stone seat where Laura and I had watched the fading landscape. Then I noticed that the door of the church was open, and I blamed myself for having left it unlatched the other night. We were the only people who ever cared to come to the church except on Sundays, and I was vexed to think that through our carelessness the damp autumn airs had had a chance of getting in and injuring the old fabric. I went in. It will seem strange, perhaps, that I should have gone half-way up the aisle before I remembered--with a sudden chill, followed by as sudden a rush of self-contempt--that this was the very day and hour when, according to tradition, the "shapes drawed out man-size in marble" began to walk.

Having thus remembered the legend, and remembered it with a shiver, of which I was ashamed, I could not do otherwise than walk up towards the altar, just to look at the figures--as I said to myself; really what I wanted was to assure myself, first, that I did not believe the legend, and, secondly, that it was not true. I was rather glad that I had come. I thought now I could tell Mrs. Dorman how vain her fancies were, and how peacefully the marble figures slept on through the ghastly hour. With my hands in my pockets I passed up the aisle. In the grey dim light the eastern end of the church looked larger than usual, and the arches above the two tombs looked larger too. The moon came out and showed me the reason. I stopped short, my heart gave a leap that nearly choked me, and then sank sickeningly.

The "bodies drawed out man-size" were gone, and their marble slabs lay wide and bare in the vague moonlight that slanted through the east window.

Were they really gone? or was I mad? Clenching my nerves, I stooped and passed my hand over the smooth slabs, and felt their flat unbroken surface. Had some one taken the things away? Was it some vile practical joke? I would make sure, anyway. In an instant I had made a torch of a newspaper, which happened to be in my pocket, and lighting it held it high above my head. Its yellow glare illumined the dark arches and those slabs. The figures were gone. And I was alone in the church; or was I alone?

And then a horror seized me, a horror indefinable and indescribable--an overwhelming certainty of supreme and accomplished calamity. I flung down the torch and tore along the aisle and out through the porch, biting my lips as I ran to keep myself from shrieking aloud. Oh, was I mad--or what was this that possessed me? I leaped the churchyard wall and took the straight cut across the fields, led by the light from our windows. Just as I got over the first stile, a dark figure seemed to spring out of the ground. Mad still with that certainty of misfortune, I made for the thing that stood in my path, shouting, "Get out of the way, can't you!"

But my push met with a more vigorous resistance than I had expected. My arms were caught just above the elbow and held as in a vice, and the raw-boned Irish doctor actually shook me.

"Would ye?" he cried, in his own unmistakable accents-- "would ye, then?"

"Let me go, you fool," I gasped. "The marble figures have gone from the church; I tell you they've gone."

He broke into a ringing laugh. "I'll have to give ye a draught to-morrow, I see. Ye've bin smoking too much and listening to old wives' tales."

"I tell you, I've seen the bare slabs."

"Well, come back with me. I'm going up to old Palmer's-- his daughter's ill; we'll look in at the church and let me see the bare slabs."

"You go, if you like," I said, a little less frantic for his laughter; "I'm going home to my wife."

"Rubbish, man," said he; "d'ye think I'll permit of that? Are ye to go saying all yer life that ye've seen solid marble endowed with vitality, and me to go all me life saying ye were a coward? No, sir--ye shan't do ut."

The night air--a human voice--and I think also the physical contact with this six feet of solid common sense, brought me back a little to my ordinary self, and the word "coward" was a mental shower-bath.

"Come on, then," I said sullenly; "perhaps you're right."

He still held my arm tightly. We got over the stile and back to the church. All was still as death. The place smelt very damp and earthy. We walked up the aisle. I am not ashamed to confess that I shut my eyes: I knew the figures would not be there. I heard Kelly strike a match.

"Here they are, ye see, right enough; ye've been dreaming or drinking, asking yer pardon for the imputation."

I opened my eyes. By Kelly's expiring vesta I saw two shapes lying "in their marble" on their slabs. I drew a deep breath, and caught his hand.

"I'm awfully indebted to you," I said. "It must have been some trick of light, or I have been working rather hard, perhaps that's it. Do you know, I was quite convinced they were gone."

"I'm aware of that," he answered rather grimly; "ye'll have to be careful of that brain of yours, my friend, I assure ye."

He was leaning over and looking at the right-hand figure, whose stony face was the most villainous and deadly in expression.

"By Jove," he said, "something has been afoot here--this hand is broken."

And so it was. I was certain that it had been perfect the last time Laura and I had been there.

"Perhaps some one has tried to remove them," said the young doctor.

"That won't account for my impression," I objected.

"Too much painting and tobacco will account for that, well enough."

"Come along," I said, "or my wife will be getting anxious. You'll come in and have a drop of whisky and drink confusion to ghosts and better sense to me."

"I ought to go up to Palmer's, but it's so late now I'd best leave it till the morning," he replied. "I was kept late at the Union, and I've had to see a lot of people since. All right, I'll come back with ye."

I think he fancied I needed him more than did Palmer's girl, so, discussing how such an illusion could have been possible, and deducing from this experience large generalities concerning ghostly apparitions, we walked up to our cottage. We saw, as we walked up the garden-path, that bright light streamed out of the front door, and presently saw that the parlour door was open too. Had she gone out?

"Come in," I said, and Dr. Kelly followed me into the parlour. It was all ablaze with candles, not only the wax ones, but at least a dozen guttering, glaring tallow dips, stuck in vases and ornaments in unlikely places. Light, I knew, was Laura's remedy for nervousness. Poor child! Why had I left her? Brute that I was.

We glanced round the room, and at first we did not see her. The window was open, and the draught set all the candles flaring one way. Her chair was empty and her handkerchief and book lay on the floor. I turned to the window. There, in the recess of the window, I saw her. Oh, my child, my love, had she gone to that window to watch for me? And what had come into the room behind her? To what had she turned with that look of frantic fear and horror? Oh, my little one, had she thought that it was I whose step she heard, and turned to meet--what?

She had fallen back across a table in the window, and her body lay half on it and half on the window-seat, and her head hung down over the table, the brown hair loosened and fallen to the carpet. Her lips were drawn back, and her eyes wide, wide open. They saw nothing now. What had they seen last?

The doctor moved towards her, but I pushed him aside and sprang to her; caught her in my arms and cried---

"It's all right, Laura! I've got you safe, wifie."

She fell into my arms in a heap. I clasped her and kissed her, and called her by all her pet names, but I think I knew all the time that she was dead. Her hands were tightly clenched. In one of them she held something fast. When I was quite sure that she was dead, and that nothing mattered at all any more, I let him open her hand to see what she held.

It was a grey marble finger.

"JOHN CHARRINGTON'S WEDDING"

(1891)

No one ever thought that May Forster would marry John Charrington; but he thought differently, and things which John Charrington intended had a queer way of coming to pass. He asked her to marry him before he went up to Oxford. She laughed and refused him. He asked her again next time he came home. Again she laughed, tossed her dainty blonde head and again refused. A third time he asked her; she said it was becoming a confirmed bad habit, and laughed at him more than ever.

John was not the only man who wanted to marry her: she was the belle of our village coterie, and we were all in love with her more or less; it was a sort of fashion, like masher collars or Inverness capes. Therefore we were as much annoyed as surprised when John Charrington walked into our little local Club -- we held it in a loft over the saddler's, I remember -- and invited us all to his wedding.

'Your wedding?'

'You don't mean it?'

'Who's the happy pair? When's it to be?'

John Charrington filled his pipe and lighted it before he replied. Then he said:

'I'm sorry to deprive you fellows of your only joke -- but Miss Forster and I are to be married in September.'

'You don't mean it?'

'He's got the mitten again, and it's turned his head.'

'No,' I said, rising, 'I see it's true. Lend me a pistol, someone --

or a first-class fare to the other end of Nowhere. Charrington has bewitched the only pretty girl in our twenty-mile radius. Was it mesmerism, or a love-potion, Jack?'

'Neither, sir, but a gift you'll never have -- perseverance -- and the best luck a man ever had in this world.'

There was something in his voice that silenced me, and all chaff of the other fellows failed to draw him further.

The queer thing about it was that when we congratulated Miss Forster, she blushed and smiled and dimpled, for all the world as though she were in love with him, and had been in love with him all the time. Upon my word, I think she had. Women are strange creatures.

We were all asked to the wedding. In Brixham everyone who was anybody knew everybody else who was anyone. My sisters were, I truly believe, more interested in the trousseau than the bride herself, and I was to be best man. The coming marriage was much canvassed at afternoon tea-tables, and at our little Club over the saddler's, and the question was always asked, 'Does she care for him?'

I used to ask that question myself in the early days of their engagement, but after a certain evening in August I never asked it again. I was coming home from the Club through the churchyard. Our church is on a thyme-grown hill, and the turf about it is so thick and soft that one's footsteps are noiseless.

I made no sound as I vaulted the low lichened wall, and threaded my way between the tombstones. It was at the same instant that I heard John Charrington's voice, and saw her. May was sitting on a low flat gravestone, her face turned towards the full splendour of the western sun. Its expression ended, at once and for ever, any question of love for him; it was transfigured to a beauty I should not have believed possible, even to that beautiful little face.

John lay at her feet, and it was his voice that broke the stillness of the golden August evening.

'My dear, my dear, I believe I should come back from the dead if you wanted me!'

I coughed at once to indicate my presence, and passed on into the shadow fully enlightened.

The wedding was to be early in September. Two days before I had to run up to town on business. The train was late, of course, for we are on the South-Eastern, and as I stood grumbling with my watch in my hand, whom should I see but John Charrington and May Forster. They were walking up and down the unfrequented end of the platform, arm in arm, looking into each other's eyes, careless of the sympathetic interest of the porters.

Of course I knew better than to hesitate a moment before burying myself in the booking-office, and it was not till the train drew up at the platform, that I obtrusively passed the pair with my Gladstone, and took the corner in a first-class smoking-carriage. I did this with as good an air of not seeing them as I could assume. I pride myself on my discretion, but if John were travelling alone I wanted his company. I had it.

'Hullo, old man,' came his cheery voice as he swung his bag into my carriage; 'here's luck; I was expecting a dull journey!'

'Where are you off to?' I asked, discretion still bidding me turn my eyes away, though I saw, without looking, that hers were red-rimmed.

'To old Branbridge's,' he answered, shutting the door and leaning out for a last word with his sweetheart.

'Oh, I wish you wouldn't go, John,' she was saying in a low, earnest voice. 'I feel certain something will happen.'

'Do you think I should let anything happen to keep me, and the day after tomorrow our wedding day?'

'Don't go,' she answered, with a pleading intensity which would have sent my Gladstone onto the platform and me after it. But she wasn't speaking to me. John Charrington was made differently: he rarely changed his opinions, never his resolutions.

He only stroked the little ungloved hands that lay on the carriage door.

'I must, May. The old boy's been awfully good to me, and now he's dying I must go and see him, but I shall come home in time for ----' the rest of the parting was lost in a whisper and in the rattling lurch of the starting train.

'You're sure to come?' she spoke as the train moved.

'Nothing shall keep me,' he answered; and we steamed out. After he had seen the last of the little figure on the platform he leaned back in his corner and kept silence for a minute.

When he spoke it was to explain to me that his godfather, whose heir he was, lay dying at Peasmarsh Place, some fifty miles away, and had sent for John, and John had felt bound to go.

'I shall be surely back tomorrow,' he said, 'or, if not, the day after, in heaps of time. Thank heaven, one hasn't to get up in the middle of the night to get married nowadays!'

'And suppose Mr Branbridge dies?'

'Alive or dead I mean to be married on Thursday!' John answered, lighting a cigar and unfolding The Times.

At Peasmarsh station we said 'goodbye', and he got out, and I saw him ride off; I went on to London, where I stayed the night.

When I got home the next afternoon, a very wet one, by the way, my sister greeted me with:

'Where's Mr Charrington?'

'Goodness knows,' I answered testily. Every man, since Cain, has resented that kind of question.

'I thought you might have heard from him,' she went on, 'as you're to give him away tomorrow.'

'Isn't he back?' I asked, for I had confidently expected to find him at home.

'No, Geoffrey,' my sister Fanny always had a way of jumping to conclusions, especially such conclusions as were least favourable to her fellow-creatures -- 'he has not returned, and, what is more, you may depend upon it he won't. You mark my words, there'll be no wedding tomorrow.'

My sister Fanny has a power of annoying me which no other human being possesses.

'You mark my words,' I retorted with asperity, 'you had better give up making such a thundering idiot of yourself. There'll be more wedding tomorrow than ever you'll take the first part in.' A prophecy which, by the way, came true.

But though I could snarl confidently to my sister, I did not feel so comfortable when late that night, I, standing on the doorstep of John's house, heard that he had not returned. I went home gloomily through the rain. Next morning brought a brilliant blue sky, gold sun, and all such softness of air and beauty of cloud as go to make up a perfect day. I woke with a vague feeling of having gone to bed anxious, and of being rather averse to facing that anxiety in the light of full wakefulness.

But with my shaving-water came a note from John which relieved my mind and sent me up to the Forsters with a light heart.

May was in the garden. I saw her blue gown through the hollyhocks as the lodge gates swung to behind me. So I did not go up to the house, but turned aside down the turfed path.

'He's written to you too,' she said, without preliminary greeting, when I reached her side.

'Yes, I'm to meet him at the station at three, and come straight on to the church.'

Her face looked pale, but there was a brightness in her eyes, and a tender quiver about the mouth that spoke of renewed happiness.

'Mr Branbridge begged him so to stay another night that he had not the heart to refuse,' she went on. 'He is so kind, but I wish he hadn't stayed.'

I was at the station at half past two. I felt rather annoyed with John. It seemed a sort of slight to the beautiful girl who loved him, that he should come as it were out of breath, and with the dust of travel upon him, to take her hand, which some of us would have given the best years of our lives to take.

But when the three o'clock train glided in, and glided out again having brought no passengers to our little station, I was more than annoyed. There was no other train for thirty-five minutes; I calculated that, with much hurry, we might just get to the church in time for the ceremony; but, oh, what a fool to miss that first train! What other man could have done it?

That thirty-five minutes seemed a year, as I wandered round the station reading the advertisements and the timetables, and the company's bye-laws, and getting more and more angry with John Charrington. This confidence in his own power of getting everything he wanted the minute he wanted it was leading him too far. I hate waiting. Everyone does, but I believe I hate it more than anyone else. The three thirty-five was late, of course.

I ground my pipe between my teeth and stamped with impatience as I watched the signals. Click. The signal went down. Five minutes later I flung myself into the carriage that I had brought for John.

'Drive to the church!' I said, as someone shut the door. 'Mr Charrington hasn't come by this train.'

Anxiety now replaced anger. What had become of the man? Could he have been taken suddenly ill? I had never known him have a day's illness in his life. And even so he might have telegraphed. Some awful accident must have happened to him. The thought that he had played her false never -- no, not for a moment -- entered my head. Yes, some thing terrible had happened to him, and on me lay the task of telling his bride. I almost wished the carriage would upset and break my head so that someone else might tell her, not I, who -- but that's nothing to do with this story.

It was five minutes to four as we drew up at the churchyard gate. A double row of eager onlookers lined the path from lychgate to porch. I sprang from the carriage and passed up between them. Our gardener had a good front place near the door. I stopped.

'Are they waiting still, Byles?' I asked, simply to gain time, for of course I knew they were by the waiting crowd's attentive attitude.

'Waiting, sir? No, no, sir; why, it must be over by now.'

'Over! Then Mr Charrington's come?'

'To the minute, sir; must have missed you somehow, and I say, sir,' lowering his voice, 'I never see Mr John the least bit so afore, but my opinion is he's been drinking pretty free. His clothes was all dusty and his face like a sheet. I tell you I didn't like the looks of him at all, and the folks inside are saying all sorts of things. You'll see, something's gone very wrong with Mr John, and he's tried liquor. He looked like a ghost, and in he went with his eyes straight before him, with never a look or a word for none of us: him that was always such a gentleman!'

I had never heard Byles make so long a speech. The crowd in the churchyard were talking in whispers and getting ready rice and slippers to throw at the bride and bridegroom. The ringers were ready with their hands on the ropes to ring out the merry peal as the bride and bridegroom should come out.

A murmur from the church announced them; out they came. Byles was right. John Charrington did not look himself. There was dust on his coat, his hair was disarranged. He seemed to have been in some row, for there was a black mark above his eyebrow. He was deathly pale. But his pallor was not greater than that of the bride, who might have been carved in ivory -- dress, veil, orange blossoms, face and all.

As they passed out the ringers stooped -- there were six of them -- and then, on the ears expecting the gay wedding peal, came the slow tolling of the passing bell.

A thrill of horror at so foolish a jest from the ringers passed through us all. But the ringers themselves dropped the ropes and fled like rabbits out into the sunlight. The bride shuddered, and grey shadows came about her mouth, but the bridegroom led her on down the path where the people stood with the handfuls of rice; but the handfuls were never thrown, and the wedding bells never rang. In vain the ringers were urged to remedy their mistake: they protested with many whispered expletives that they would see themselves further first.

In a hush like the hush in the chamber of death the bridal pair passed into their carriage and its door slammed behind them.

Then the tongues were loosed. A babel of anger, wonder, conjecture from the guests and the spectators.

'If I'd seen his condition, sir,' said old Forster to me as we drove off, 'I would have stretched him on the floor of the church, sir, by heaven I would, before I'd have let him marry my daughter!'

Then he put his head out of the window.

'Drive like hell,' he cried to the coachman; 'don't spare the horses.'

He was obeyed. We passed the bride's carriage. I forbore to look at it, and old Forster turned his head away and swore. We reached home before it.

We stood in the doorway, in the blazing afternoon sun, and in about half a minute we heard wheels crunching the gravel. When the carriage stopped in front of the steps old Forster and I ran down.

'Great heaven, the carriage is empty! And yet ----'

I had the door open in a minute, and this is what I saw ...

No sign of John Charrington; and of May, his wife, only a huddled heap of white satin lying half on the floor of the carriage and half on the seat.

'I drove straight here, sir,' said the coachman, as the bride's father lifted her out; 'and I'll swear no one got out of the carriage.'

We carried her into the house in her bridal dress and drew back her veil. I saw her face. Shall I ever forget it? White, white and drawn with agony and horror, bearing such a look of terror as I have never seen since except in dreams. And her hair, her radiant blonde hair, I tell you it was white like snow.

As we stood, her father and I, half mad with the horror and mystery of it, a boy came up the avenue -- a telegraph boy. They brought the orange envelope to me. I tore it open.

Mr Charrington was thrown from the dogcart on his way to the station at half past one. Killed on the spot!

And he was married to May Forster in our parish church at half past three, in presence of half the parish.

'I shall be married, dead, or alive!'

What had passed in that carriage on the homeward drive? No one knows -- no one will ever know. Oh, May! oh, my dear!

Before a week was over they laid her beside her husband in our little churchyard on the thyme-covered hill -- the churchyard where they had kept their love-trysts.

Thus was accomplished John Charrington's wedding.

THE TWO PENNY SPELL

Lucy was a very good little girl indeed, and Harry was not so bad—for a boy, though the grown-ups called him a limb! They both got on very well at school, and were not wholly unloved at home. Perhaps Lucy was a bit of a muff, and Harry was certainly very rude to call her one, but she need not have replied by calling him a 'beast.' I think she did it partly to show him that she was not quite so much of a muff as he thought, and partly because she was naturally annoyed at being buried up to her waist in the ground among the gooseberry-bushes. She got into the hole Harry had dug because he said it might make her grow, and then he suddenly shovelled down a heap of earth and stamped it down so that she could not move. She began to cry, then he said 'muff' and she said 'beast,' and he went away and left her 'planted there,' as the French people say. And she cried more than ever, and tried to dig herself out, and couldn't, and although she was naturally such a gentle child, she would have stamped with rage, only she couldn't get her feet out to do it. Then she screamed, and her Uncle Richard came and dug her out, and said it was a shame, and gave her twopence to spend as she liked. So she got nurse to clean the gooseberry ground off her, and when she was cleaned she went out to spend the twopence. She was allowed to go alone, because the shops were only a little way off on the same side of the road, so there was no danger from crossings.

'I'll spend every penny of it on myself,' said Lucy savagely; 'Harry shan't have a bit, unless I could think of something he wouldn't like, and then I'd get it and put it in his bread and milk!' She had never felt quite so spiteful before, but, then, Harry had never before been quite so aggravating.

She walked slowly along by the shops, wishing she could think of something that Harry hated; she herself hated worms, but Harry didn't mind them. Boys are so odd.

Suddenly she saw a shop she had never noticed before. The window was quite full of flowers—roses, lilies, violets, pinks, pansies—everything you can think of, growing in a tangled heap, as you see them in an old garden in July.

She looked for the name over the shop. Instead of being somebody or other, Florist, it was 'Doloro de Lara, Professor of white and black Magic,' and in the window was a large card, framed and glazed. It said:

ENCHANTMENTS DONE WHILE YOU WAIT.

EVERY DESCRIPTION OF CHARM CAREFULLY AND COMPETENTLY WORKED. STRONG SPELLS FROM FIFTY GUINEAS TO TUPPENCE. WE SUIT ALL PURSES. GIVE US A TRIAL. BEST AND CHEAPEST HOUSE IN THE TRADE.

COMPETITION DEFIED.

Lucy read this with her thumb in her mouth. It was the tuppence that attracted her; she had never bought a spell, and even a tuppenny one would be something new.

'It's some sort of conjuring trick, I suppose,' she thought, 'and I'll never let Harry see how it's done—never, never, never!'

She went in. The shop was just as flowery, and bowery, and red-rosy, and white-lilyish inside as out, and the colour and the scent almost took her breath away. A thin, dark, unpleasing gentleman suddenly popped out of a bower of flowering nightshade, and said:

'And what can we do for you to-day, miss?'

'I want a spell, if you please,' said Lucy; 'the best you can do for tuppence.'

'Is that all you've got?' said he.

'Yes,' said Lucy.

'Well, you can't expect much of a spell for that,' said he;

'however, it's better that I should have the tuppence than that you should; you see that, of course. Now, what would you like? We can do you a nice little spell at sixpence that'll make it always jam for tea. And I've another article at eighteenpence that'll make the grown-ups always think you're good even if you're not; and at half a crown——'

"'And what can we do for you to-day, Miss?'"

'I've only got tuppence.'

'Well,' he said crossly, 'there's only one spell at that price, and that's really a tuppenny-half-penny one; but we'll say tuppence. I can make you like somebody else, and somebody else like you.'

'Thank you,' said Lucy; 'I like most people, and everybody likes me.'

'I don't mean *that*,' he said. 'Isn't there someone you'd like to hurt if you were as strong as they are, and they were as weak as you?'

'Yes,' said Lucy in a guilty whisper.

'Then hand over your tuppence,' said the dark gentleman, 'and it's a bargain.'

He snatched the coppers warm from her hand.

'Now,' he said, 'to-morrow morning you'll be as strong as Harry, and he'll be little and weak like you. Then you can hurt him as much as you like, and he won't be able to hurt back.'

'Oh!' said Lucy; 'but I'm not sure I want——I think I'd like to change the spell, please.'

'No goods exchanged,' he said crossly; 'you've got what you asked for.'

'Thank you,' said Lucy doubtfully, 'but how am I——?'

'It's entirely self-adjusting,' said nasty Mr. Doloro. 'No previous experience required.'

'Thank you very much,' said Lucy. 'Good——'

She was going to say 'good-morning,' but it turned into 'good gracious,' because she was so very much astonished. For, without a moment's warning, the flower-shop had turned into the sweet-shop that she knew so well, and nasty Mr. Doloro had turned into the sweet-woman, who was asking what she wanted, to which, of course, as she had spent her twopence, the answer was 'Nothing.' She was already sorry that she had spent it, and in such a way, and she was sorrier still when she got home, and Harry owned handsomely that *he* was sorry he had planted her out, but he really hadn't thought she was such a little idiot, and he *was* sorry—so there! This touched Lucy's heart, and she felt more than ever that she had not laid out her tuppence to the best advantage. She tried to warn Harry of what was to happen in the morning, but he only said, 'Don't yarn; Billson Minor's coming for cricket. You can field if you like.' Lucy didn't like, but it seemed the only thing she could do to show that she accepted in a proper spirit her brother's apology about the planting out. So she fielded gloomily and ineffectively.

Next morning Harry got up in good time, folded up his nightshirt, and made his room so tidy that the housemaid nearly had a surprise-fit when she went in. He crept downstairs like a mouse, and learned his lessons before breakfast. Lucy, on the other hand, got up so late that it was only by dressing hastily that she had time to prepare a thoroughly good booby-trap before she slid down the banisters just as the breakfast-bell rang. She was first in the room, so she was able to put a little salt in all the tea-cups before anyone else came in. Fresh tea was made, and Harry was blamed. Lucy said, 'I did it,' but no one believed her. They said she was a noble, unselfish sister to try and shield her naughty brother, and Harry burst into floods of tears when she kicked him under the table; she hated herself for doing this, but somehow it seemed impossible to do anything else.

Harry cried nearly all the way to school, while Lucy insisted on sliding along all the gutters and dragging Harry after her. She bought a catapult at the toy-shop and a pennyworth of tintacks at the oil-shop, both on credit, and as Lucy had never asked for credit before, she got it.

At the top of Blackheath Village they separated—Harry went back to his school, which is at the other side of the station, and Lucy went on to the High School.

The Blackheath High School has a large and beautiful hall, with a staircase leading down into it like a staircase in a picture, and at the other end of the hall is a big statue of a beautiful lady. The High School mistresses call her Venus, but I don't really believe that is her name.

Lucy—good, gentle, little Lucy, beloved by her form mistress and respected by all the school—sat on those steps—I don't know why no one caught her—and used her catapult to throw ink pellets (you know what they are, of course) with her catapult at the beautiful white statue-lady, till the Venus—if that is her name, which I doubt—was all over black spots, like a Dalmation or carriage dog.

Then she went into her class room and arranged tintacks, with the business end up, on all the desks and seats, an act fraught with gloomy returns to Blossoma Rand and Wilhelmina Marguerite Asterisk. Another booby-trap—a dictionary, a pot of water, three pieces of chalk, and a handful of torn paper—was hastily sketched above the door. Three other little girls looked on in open-mouthed appreciation. I do not wish to shock you, so I will not tell you about the complete success of the booby-trap, nor of the bloodthirsty fight between Lucy and Bertha Kaurter in a secluded fives-court during rec. Dora Spielman and Gertrude Rook were agitated seconds. It was Lucy's form mistress, the adored Miss Harter Larke, who interrupted the fight at the fifth round, and led the blood-stained culprits into the hall and up the beautiful picture-like steps to the Headmistress's room.

The Head of the Blackheath High School has all the subtle generalship of the Head in Mr. Kipling's 'Stalky.' She has also a manner which subdues parents and children alike to 'what she works in, like the dyer's hand.' Anyone less clever would have expelled the luckless Lucy—saddled with her brother's boy-nature—on such evidence as was now brought forward. Not so the Blackheath Head. She reserved judgment, the most terrible of all things for a culprit, by the way, who thought it over for an hour and a half in the mistress's room, and she privately wrote a note to Lucy's mother, gently hinting that Lucy was not quite herself: might be sickening for something. Perhaps she had better be kept at home for a day or two. Lucy went home, and on the way upset a bicycle with a little girl on it, and came off best in a heated physical argument with a baker's boy.

Harry, meanwhile, had dried his tears, and gone to school.

He knew his lessons, which was a strange and pleasing thing, and roused in his master hopes destined to be firmly and thoroughly crushed in the near future. But when he had emerged triumphantly from morning school he suddenly found his head being punched by Simpkins Minor, on the ground that he, Harry, had been showing off. The punching was scientific and irresistible. Harry, indeed, did not try to resist; in floods of tears and with uncontrolled emotion he implored Simpkins Minor to let him alone, and not be a brute. Then Simpkins Minor kicked him, and several other nice little boy-friends of his joined the glad throng, and it became quite a kicking party. So that when Harry and Lucy met at the corner of Wemyss Road his face was almost unrecognisable, while Lucy looked as happy as a king, and as proud as a peacock.

'What's up?' asked Lucy briskly.

'Every single boy in the school has kicked me,' said Harry in flat accents. 'I wish I was dead.'

'So do I,' said Lucy cheerily; 'I think I'm going to be expelled. I should be quite certain, only my booby-trap came down on Bessie Jayne's head instead of Miss Whatshername's, and Bessie's no sneak, though she has got a lump like an ostrich's egg on her forehead, and soaked through as well. But I think I'm certain to be expelled.'

'I wish I was,' said Harry, weeping with heartfelt emotion. 'I don't know what's the matter with me; I feel all wrong inside. Do you think you can turn into things just by reading them? Because I feel as if I was in "Sandford and Merton," or one of the books the kind clergyman lent us at the seaside.'

'How awfully beastly!' said Lucy. 'Now, I feel as if I didn't care tuppence whether I was expelled or not. And, I say, Harry, I feel as if I was much stronger than you. I know I could twist your arm round and then hit it like you did me the other day, and you couldn't stop me.'

'Of course I couldn't! *I* can't stop anybody doing anything they want to do. Anybody who likes can hit me, and I can't hit back.'

He began to cry again. And suddenly Lucy was really sorry. She had done this, she had degraded her happy brother to a mere milksop, just because he had happened to plant her out, and leave her planted. Remorse suddenly gripped her with tooth and claw.

'Look here,' she said, 'it's all my fault! Because you planted me out, and I wanted to hurt you. But now I don't. I can't make you boy-brave again; but I'm sorry, and I'll look after you, Harry, old man! Perhaps you could disguise yourself in frocks and long hair, and come to the High School. I'd take care nobody bullied you. It isn't nice being bullied, is it?'

Harry flung his arms round her, a thing he would never have done in the public street if he had not been girlish inside at the time.

'No, it's hateful,' he said. 'Lucy, I'm sorry I've been such a pig to you.'

Lucy put her arms round him, and they kissed each other, though it was broad daylight and they were walking down Lee Park.

The same moment the enchanter Doloro de Lara ran into them on the pavement. Lucy screamed, and Harry hit out as hard as he could.

'Look out,' said he; 'who are you shoving into?'

'Tut-tut,' said the enchanter, putting his hat straight, 'you've bust up your spell, my Lucy—child; no spells hold if you go kissing and saying you're sorry. Just keep that in mind for the future, will you?'

He vanished in the white cloud of a passing steam-motor, and Harry and Lucy were left looking at each other. And Harry was Harry and Lucy was Lucy to the very marrow of their little backbones. They shook hands with earnest feeling.

Next day Lucy went to the High School and apologised in dust and ashes.

'I don't think I was my right self,' she said to the Headmistress, who quite agreed with her, 'and I never will again!'

And she never has. Harry, on the other hand, thrashed

Simpkins Minor thoroughly and scientifically on the first opportunity; but he did not thrash him extravagantly: he tempered pluck with mercy.

For this is the odd thing about the whole story. Ever since the day when the tuppenny spell did its work Harry has been kinder than before and Lucy braver. I can't think why, but so it is. He no longer bullies her, and she is no longer afraid of him, and every time she does something brave for him, or he does something kind for her, they grow more and more alike, so that when they are grown up he may as well be called Lucius and she Harriett, for all the difference there will be between them.

And all the grown-ups look on and admire, and think that their incessant jawing has produced this improvement. And no one suspects the truth except the Headmistress of the High School, who has gone through the complete course of Social Magic under a better professor than Mr. Doloro de Lara; that is why she understands everything, and why she did not expel Lucy, but only admonished her. Harry is cock of his school now, and Lucy is in the sixth, and a model girl. I wish all Headmistresses learned Magic at Girton.

A COURSE IN MAGIC.

THERE was once a lady who found herself in middle life with but a slight income. Knowing herself to be insufficiently educated to be able to practise any other trade or calling, she of course decided, without hesitation, to enter the profession of teaching. She opened a very select Boarding School for Young Ladies. The highest references were given and required. And in order to keep her school as select as possible, Miss Fitzroy Robinson had a brass plate fastened on to the door, with an inscription in small polite lettering. (You have, of course, heard of the "polite letters." Well, it was with these that Miss Fitzroy Robinson's door-plate was engraved.)

"SELECT BOARDING ESTABLISHMENT FOR THE DAUGHTERS OF RESPECTABLE MONARCHS."

A great many kings who were not at all respectable would have given their royal ears to be allowed to send their daughters to this school, but Miss Fitzroy Robinson was very firm about references, and the consequence was that all the really high-class kings were only too pleased to be permitted to pay ten thousand pounds a year for their daughters' education. And so Miss Fitzroy Robinson was able to lay aside a few pounds as a provision for her old age. And all the money she saved was invested in land.

Only one monarch refused to send his daughter to Miss Fitzroy Robinson, on the ground that so cheap a school could not be a really select one, and it was found out afterwards that his references were not at all satisfactory.

There were only six boarders, and of course the best masters were engaged to teach the royal pupils everything which their parents wished them to learn, and as the girls were never asked to do lessons except when they felt quite inclined, they all said it was the nicest school in the world, and cried at the very thought of being taken away. Thus it happened that the six pupils were quite grown up and were just becoming parlour boarders when events began to occur. Princess Daisy, the daughter of King Fortunatus, the ruling sovereign, was the only little girl in the school.

Now it was when she had been at school about a year, that a ring came at the front door-bell, and the maid-servant came to the schoolroom with a visiting card held in the corner of her apron—for her hands were wet because it was washing-day.

"A gentleman to see you, Miss," she said; and Miss Fitzroy Robinson was quite fluttered because she thought it might be a respectable monarch, with a daughter who wanted teaching.

But when she looked at the card she left off fluttering, and said, "Dear me!" under her breath, because she was very genteel. If she had been vulgar like some of us she would have said "Bother!" and if she had been more vulgar than, I hope, any of us are, she might have said "Drat the man!" The card was large and shiny and had gold letters on it. Miss Fitzroy Robinson read:—

>Chevalier Doloro De Lara
>Professor of Magic (white) and the Black Art.
>Pupils instructed at their own residences.
>No extras.
>Special terms for Schools. Evening Parties attended.

Miss Fitzroy Robinson laid down her book—she never taught without a book—smoothed her yellow cap and her grey curls and went into the front parlour to see her visitor. He bowed low at sight of her. He was very tall and hungry-looking, with black eyes, and an indescribable mouth.

"It is indeed a pleasure," said he, smiling so as to show every one of his thirty-two teeth—a very polite, but very difficult thing to do—"it is indeed a pleasure to meet once more my old pupil."

"The pleasure is mutual, I am sure," said Miss Fitzroy Robinson. If it is sometimes impossible to be polite and truthful at the same moment, that is not my fault, nor Miss Fitzroy Robinson's.

"I have been travelling about," said the Professor, still smiling immeasurably, "increasing my stock of wisdom. Ah, dear lady—we live and learn, do we not? And now I am really a far more competent teacher than when I had the honour of instructing you. May I hope for an engagement as Professor in your Academy?"

"I have not yet been able to arrange for a regular course of Magic," said the schoolmistress; "it is a subject in which parents, especially royal ones, take but too little interest."

"It was your favourite study," said the professor.

"Yes—but—well, no doubt some day——"

"But I want an engagement *now*," said he, looking hungrier than ever; "a thousand pounds for thirteen lessons—to *you*, dear lady."

"It's quite impossible," said she, and she spoke firmly, for she knew from history how dangerous it is for a Magician to be allowed anywhere near a princess. Some harm almost always comes of it.

"Oh, very well!" said the Professor.

"You see my pupils are all princesses," she went on, "they don't require the use of magic, they can get all they want without it."

"Then it's 'No'?" said he.

"It's 'No thank you kindly,'" said she.

Then, before she could stop him, he sprang past her out at the door, and she heard his boots on the oilcloth of the passage. She flew after him just in time to have the schoolroom door slammed and locked in her face.

"Well, I never!" said Miss Fitzroy Robinson. She hastened to the top of the house and hurried down the schoolroom chimney, which had been made with steps, in case of fire or other emergency. She stepped out of the grate on to the schoolroom hearthrug just one second too late. The seven Princesses were all gone, and the Professor of Magic stood alone among the inkstained desks, smiling the largest smile Miss Fitzroy Robinson had seen yet.

"Oh, you naughty, bad, wicked man, you!" said she, shaking the school ruler at him.

* * * * *

The next day was Saturday, and the King of the country called as usual to take his daughter Daisy out to spend her half holiday. The servant who opened the door had a coarse apron on and cinders in her hair, and the King thought it was sackcloth and ashes, and said so a little anxiously, but the girl said, "No, I've only been a-doing of the kitchen range—though, for the matter of that—but you'd best see missus herself."

So the King was shown into the best parlour where the tasteful wax-flowers were, and the antimacassars and water-colour drawings executed by the pupils, and the wool mats which Miss Fitzroy Robinson's bed-ridden aunt made so beautifully. A delightful parlour full of the traces of the refining touch of a woman's hand.

Miss Fitzroy Robinson came in slowly and sadly. Her gown was neatly made of sack-cloth—with an ingenious trimming of small cinders sewn on gold braid—and some larger-sized cinders dangled by silken threads from the edge of her lace cap.

The King saw at once that she was annoyed about something. "I hope I'm not too early," said he.

"Your Majesty," she answered, "not at all. You are always punctual, as stated in your references. Something has happened. I will not aggravate your misfortunes by breaking them to you. Your daughter Daisy, the pride and treasure of our little circle, has disappeared. Her six royal companions are with her. For the present all are safe, but at the moment I am unable to lay my hand on any one of the seven."

The King sat down heavily on part of the handsome walnut and rep suite (ladies' and gentlemen's easy-chairs, couch and six occasional chairs) and gasped miserably. He could not find words. But the schoolmistress had written down what she was going to say on a slate and learned it off by heart, so she was able to go on fluently.

"Your Majesty, I am not wholly to blame—hang me if I am—I mean hang me if you must; but first allow me to have the honour of offering to you one or two explanatory remarks."

With this she sat down and told him the whole story of the Professor's visit, only stopping exactly where I stopped when I was telling it to you just now.

The King listened, plucking nervously at the fringe of a purple and crimson antimacassar.

"I never *was* satisfied with the Professor's methods," said Miss Fitzroy Robinson sadly; "and I always had my doubts as to his moral character, doubts now set at rest for ever. After concluding my course of instruction with him some years ago I took a series of lessons from a far more efficient master, and thanks to those lessons, which were, I may mention, extremely costly, I was mercifully enabled to put a spoke in the wheel of the unprincipled ruffian——"

"Did you save the Princesses?" cried the King.

"No; but I can if your Majesty and the other parents will leave the matter entirely in my hands."

"It's rather a serious matter," said the King; "my poor little Daisy——"

"I would ask you," said the schoolmistress with dignity, "not to attach too much importance to this event. Of course it is regrettable, but unpleasant accidents occur in all schools, and the consequences of them can usually be averted by the exercise of tact and judgment."

"I ought to hang you, you know," said the King doubtfully.

"No doubt," said Miss Fitzroy Robinson, "and if you do you'll never see your Daisy again. Your duty as a parent—yes—and your duty to me—conflicting duties are very painful things."

"But can I trust you?"

"I may remind you," said she, drawing herself up so that the cinders rattled again, "that we exchanged satisfactory references at the commencement of our business relations."

The King rose. "Well, Miss Fitzroy Robinson," he said, "I have been entirely satisfied with Daisy's progress since she has been in your charge, and I feel I cannot do better than leave this matter entirely in your able hands."

The schoolmistress made him a curtsey, and he went back to his marble palace a broken-hearted monarch, with his crown all on one side and his poor, dear nose red with weeping.

The select boarding establishment was shut up.

Time went on and no news came of the lost Princesses.

The King found but little comfort in the fact that his other child, Prince Denis, was still spared to him. Denis was all very well and a nice little boy in his way, but a boy is not a girl.

The Queen was much more broken-hearted than the King, but of course she had the housekeeping to see to and the making of the pickles and preserves and the young Prince's stockings to knit, so she had not much time for weeping, and after a year she said to the King—

"My dear, you ought to do something to distract your mind. It's unkinglike to sit and cry all day. Now, do make an effort; do something useful, if it's only opening a bazaar or laying a foundation stone."

"I am frightened of bazaars," said the King; "they are like bees—they buzz and worry; but foundation stones——" And after that he began to sit and think sometimes, without crying, and to make notes on the backs of old envelopes. So the Queen felt that she had not spoken quite in vain.

A month later the suggestion of foundation stones bore fruit.

The King floated a company, and Fortunatus Rex & Co. became almost at once the largest speculative builders in the world.

Perhaps you do not know what a speculative builder is. I'll tell you what the King and his Co. did, and then you will know.

They bought all the pretty woods and fields they could get and cut them up into squares, and grubbed up the trees and the grass and put streets there and lamp-posts and ugly little yellow brick houses, in the hopes that people would want to live in them. And curiously enough people did. So the King and his Co. made quite a lot of money.

It is curious that nearly all the great fortunes are made by turning beautiful things into ugly ones. Making beauty out of ugliness is very ill-paid work.

The ugly little streets crawled further and further out of the town, eating up the green country like greedy yellow caterpillars, but at the foot of the Clover Hill they had to stop. For the owner of Clover Hill would not sell any land at all—for any price that Fortunatus Rex & Co. could offer. In vain the solicitors of the Company called on the solicitors of the owner, wearing their best cloaks and swords and shields, and took them out to lunch and gave them nice things to eat and drink. Clover Hill was not for sale.

At last, however, a little old woman all in grey called at the Company's shining brass and mahogany offices and had a private interview with the King himself.

"I am the owner of Clover Hill," said she, "and you may build on all its acres except the seven at the top and the fifteen acres that go round that seven, and you must build me a high wall round the seven acres and another round the fifteen—of *red* brick, mind; none of your cheap yellow stuff—and you must make a brand new law that any one who steals my fruit is to be hanged from the tree he stole it from. That's all. What do you say?"

The King said "Yes," because since his trouble he cared for nothing but building, and his royal soul longed to see the green Clover Hill eaten up by yellow brick caterpillars with slate tops. He did not at all like building the two red brick walls, but he did it.

Now, the old woman wanted the walls and the acres to be this sort of shape—

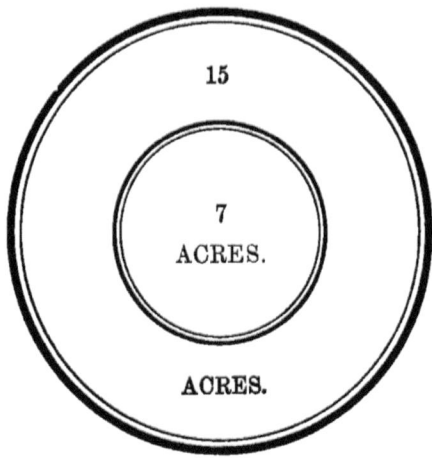

But it was such a bother getting the exact amount of ground into the two circles that all the surveyors tore out their hair by handfuls, and at last the King said, "Oh bother! Do it this way," and drew a plan on the back of an old Act of Parliament. So they did, and it was like this—

The old lady was very vexed when she found that there was only one wall between her orchard and the world, as you see was the case at the corner where the two 1's and the 15 meet; but the King said he couldn't afford to build it all over again and that she'd got her two walls as she had said.

So she had to put up with it. Only she insisted on the King's getting her a fierce bull-dog to fly at the throat of any one who should come over the wall at that weak point where the two 1's join on to the 15. So he got her a stout bull-dog whose name was Martha, and brought it himself in a jewelled leash.

"Martha will fly at any one who is not of kingly blood," said he. "Of course she wouldn't dream of biting a royal person; but, then, on the other hand, royal people don't rob orchards."

So the old woman had to be contented. She tied Martha up in the unprotected corner of her inner enclosure and then she planted little baby apple trees and had a house built and sat down in it and waited.

And the King was almost happy. The creepy, crawly yellow caterpillars ate up Clover Hill—all except the little green crown on the top, where the apple trees were and the two red brick walls and the little house and the old woman.

The poor Queen went on seeing to the jam and the pickles and the blanket washing and the spring cleaning, and every now and then she would say to her husband—

"Fortunatus, my love, do you *really* think Miss Fitzroy Robinson is trustworthy? Shall we ever see our Daisy again?"

And the King would rumple his fair hair with his hands till it stuck out like cheese straws under his crown, and answer—

"My dear, you must be patient; you know we had the very highest references."

Now one day the new yellow brick town the King had built had a delightful experience. Six handsome Princes on beautiful white horses came riding through the dusty little streets. The housings of their chargers shone with silver embroidery and gleaming glowing jewels, and their gold armour flashed so gloriously in the sun that all the little children clapped their hands, and the Princes' faces were so young and kind and handsome that all the old women said: "Bless their pretty hearts!"

Now, of course, you will not need to be told that these six Princes were looking for the six grown-up Princesses who had been so happy at the Select Boarding Establishment. Their six Royal fathers, who lived many years' journey away on the other side of the world, and had not yet heard that the Princesses were mislaid, had given Miss Fitzroy Robinson's address to these Princes, and instructed them to marry the six Princesses without delay, and bring them home.

But when they got to the Select Boarding Establishment for the Daughters of Respectable Monarchs, the house was closed, and a card was in the window, saying that this desirable villa residence was to be let on moderate terms, furnished or otherwise. The wax fruit under the glass shade still showed attractively through the dusty panes. The six Princes looked through the window by turns. They were charmed with the furniture, and the refining touch of a woman's hand drew them like a magnet. They took the house, but they had their meals at the Palace by the King's special invitation.

King Fortunatus told the Princes the dreadful story of the disappearance of the entire Select School; and each Prince swore by his sword-hilt and his honour that he would find out the particular Princess that he was to marry, or perish in the attempt. For, of course, each Prince was to marry one Princess, mentioned by name in his instructions, and not one of the others.

The first night that the Princes spent in the furnished house passed quietly enough, so did the second and the third and the fourth, fifth and sixth, but on the seventh night, as the Princes sat playing spilikins in the schoolroom, they suddenly heard a voice that was not any of theirs. It said, "Open up Africa!"

The Princes looked here, there, and everywhere—but they could see no one. They had not been brought up to the exploring trade, and could not have opened up Africa if they had wanted to.

"Or cut through the Isthmus of Panama," said the voice again.

Now, as it happened, none of the six Princes were engineers. They confessed as much.

"Cut up China, then!" said the voice, desperately.

"It's like the ghost of a Tory newspaper," said one of the Princes.

And then suddenly they knew that the voice came from one of the pair of globes which hung in frames at the end of the schoolroom. It was the terrestrial globe.

"I'm inside," said the voice; "I can't get out. Oh, cut the globe—anywhere—and let me out. But the African route is most convenient."

Prince Primus opened up Africa with his sword, and out tumbled half a Professor of Magic.

"My other half's in there," he said, pointing to the Celestial globe. "Let my legs out, do——"

But Prince Secundus said, "Not so fast," and Prince Tertius said, "Why were you shut up?"

"I was shut up for as pretty a bit of parlour-magic as ever you saw in all your born days," said the top half of the Professor of Magic.

"Oh, you were, were you?" said Prince Quartus; "well, your legs aren't coming out just yet. We want to engage a competent magician. You'll do."

"But I'm not all here," said the Professor.

"Quite enough of you," said Prince Quintus.

"Now look here," said Prince Sextus; "we want to find our six Princesses. We can give a very good guess as to how they were lost; but we'll let bygones be bygones. You tell us how to find them, and after our weddings we'll restore your legs to the light of day."

"This half of me feels so faint," said the half Professor of Magic.

"What are we to do?" said all the Princes, threateningly; "if you don't tell us, you shall never have a leg to stand on."

"Steal apples," said the half Professor, hoarsely, and fainted away.

They left him lying on the bare boards between the inkstained desks, and off they went to steal apples. But this was not so easy. Because Fortunatus Rex & Co. had built, and built, and built, and apples do not grow freely in those parts of the country which have been "opened up" by speculative builders.

So at last they asked the little Prince Denis where he went for apples when he wanted them. And Denis said—

"The old woman at the top of Clover Hill has apples in her seven acres, and in her fifteen acres, but there's a fierce bulldog in the seven acres, and I've stolen all the apples in the fifteen acres myself."

"We'll try the seven acres," said the Princes.

"Very well," said Denis; "You'll be hanged if you're caught. So, as I put you up to it, I'm coming too, and if you won't take me, I'll tell. So there!"

For Denis was a most honourable little Prince, and felt that you must not send others into danger unless you go yourself, and he would never have stolen apples if it had not been quite as dangerous as leading armies.

So the Princes had to agree, and the very next night Denis let himself down out of his window by a knotted rope made of all the stockings his mother had knitted for him, and the grown-up Princes were waiting under the window, and off they all went to the orchard on the top of Clover Hill.

They climbed the wall at the proper corner, and Martha, the bulldog, who was very wellbred, and knew a Prince when she saw one, wagged her kinked tail respectfully and wished them good luck.

The Princes stole over the dewy orchard grass and looked at tree after tree: there were no apples on any of them.

Only at last, in the very middle of the orchard there was a tree with a copper trunk and brass branches, and leaves of silver. And on it hung seven beautiful golden apples.

So each Prince took one of the golden apples, very quietly, and off they went, anxious to get back to the half-Professor of Magic, and learn what to do next. No one had any doubt as to the half-Professor having told the truth; for when your legs depend on your speaking the truth you will not willingly tell a falsehood.

They stole away as quietly as they could, each with a gold apple in his hand, but as they went Prince Denis could not resist his longing to take a bite out of his apple. He opened his mouth very wide so as to get a good bite, and the next moment he howled aloud, for the apple was as hard as stone, and the poor little boy had broken nearly all his first teeth.

He flung the apple away in a rage, and the next moment the old woman rushed out of her house. She screamed. Martha barked. Prince Denis howled. The whole town was aroused, and the six Princes were arrested, and taken under a strong guard to the Tower. Denis was let off, on the ground of his youth, and, besides, he had lost most of his teeth, which is a severe punishment, even for stealing apples.

The King sat in his Hall of Justice next morning, and the old woman and the Princes came before him. When the story had been told, he said—

"My dear fellows, I hope you'll excuse me—the laws of hospitality are strict—but business is business after all. I should not like to have any constitutional unpleasantness over a little thing like this; you must all be hanged to-morrow morning."

The Princes were extremely vexed, but they did not make a fuss. They asked to see Denis, and told him what to do.

So Denis went to the furnished house which had once been a Select Boarding Establishment for the Daughters of Respectable Monarchs. The door was locked, but Denis knew a way in, because his sister had told him all about it one holiday. He got up on the roof and walked down the schoolroom chimney.

There, on the schoolroom floor, lay half a Professor of Magic, struggling feebly, and uttering sad, faint squeals.

"What are we to do now?" said Denis.

"Steal apples," said the half-Professor in a weak whisper. "Do let my legs out. Slice up the Great Bear—or the Milky Way would be a good one for them to come out by."

But Denis knew better.

"Not till we get the lost Princesses," said he, "now, what's to be done?"

"Steal apples I tell you," said the half-Professor, crossly; "seven apples—there—seven kisses. Cut them down. Oh go along with you, do. Leave me to die, you heartless boy. I've got pins and needles in my legs."

Then off ran Denis to the Seven Acre Orchard at the top of Clover Hill, and there were the six Princes hanging to the apple-tree, and the hangman had gone home to his dinner, and there was no one else about. And the Princes were not dead.

Denis climbed up the tree and cut the Princes down with the penknife of the gardener's boy. (You will often find this penknife mentioned in your German exercises; now you know why so much fuss is made about it.)

The Princes fell to the ground, and when they recovered their wits Denis told them what he had done.

"Oh why did you cut us down?" said the Princes, "we were having such happy dreams."

"Well," said Denis, shutting up the penknife of the gardener's boy, "of all the ungrateful chaps!" And he turned his back and marched off. But they ran quickly after him and thanked him and told him how they had been dreaming of walking arm in arm with the most dear and lovely Princesses in the world.

"Well," said Denis, "it's no use dreaming about *them*. You've got your own registered Princesses to find, and the half-Professor says, 'Steal apples.'"

"There aren't any more to steal," said the Princes—but when they looked, there were the gold apples back on the tree just as before.

So once again they each picked one. Denis chose a different one this time. He thought it might be softer. The last time he had chosen the biggest apple—but now he took the littlest apple of all.

"Seven kisses!" he cried, and began to kiss the little gold apple.

Each Prince kissed the apple he held, till the sound of kisses was like the whisper of the evening wind in leafy trees. And, of course, at the seventh kiss each Prince found that he had in his hand not an apple, but the fingers of a lovely Princess. As for Denis, he had got his little sister Daisy, and he was so glad he promised at once to give her his guinea-pigs and his whole collection of foreign postage stamps.

"What is your name, dear and lovely lady?" asked Prince Primus.

"Sexta," said his Princess. And then it turned out that every single one of the Princes had picked the wrong apple, so that each one had a Princess who was not the one mentioned in his letter of instructions. Secundus had plucked the apple that held Quinta, and Tertius held Quarta, and so on—and everything was as criss-cross-crooked as it possibly could be.

And yet nobody wanted to change.

Then the old woman came out of her house and looked at them and chuckled, and she said—

"You must be contented with what you have."

"We *are*," said all twelve of them, "but what about our parents?"

"They must put up with your choice," said the old woman, "it's the common lot of parents."

"I think you ought to sort yourselves out properly," said Denis; "I'm the only one who's got his right Princess—because I wasn't greedy. I took the smallest."

The tallest Princess showed him a red mark on her arm, where his little teeth had been two nights before, and everybody laughed.

But the old woman said—

"They can't change, my dear. When a Prince has picked a gold apple that has a Princess in it, and has kissed it till she comes out, no other Princess will ever do for him, any more than any other Prince will ever do for her."

While she was speaking the old woman got younger and younger and younger, till as she spoke the last words she was quite young, not more than fifty-five. And it was Miss Fitzroy Robinson!

Her pupils stepped forward one by one with respectful curtsies, and she allowed them to kiss her on the cheek, just as if it was breaking-up day.

Then, all together, and very happily, they went down to the

furnished villa that had once been the Select School, and when the half-professor had promised on his honour as a Magician to give up Magic and take to a respectable trade, they took his legs out of the starry sphere, and gave them back to him; and he joined himself together, and went off full of earnest resolve to live and die an honest plumber.

"My talents won't be quite wasted," said he; "a little hanky-panky is useful in most trades."

When the King asked Miss Fitzroy Robinson to name her own reward for restoring the Princesses, she said—

"Make the land green again, your Majesty."

So Fortunatus Rex & Co. devoted themselves to pulling down and carting off the yellow streets they had built. And now the country there is almost as green and pretty as it was before Princess Daisy and the six parlour-boarders were turned into gold apples.

"It was very clever of dear Miss Fitzroy Robinson to shut up that Professor in those two globes," said the Queen; "it shows the advantage of having lessons from the best Masters."

"Yes," said the King, "I always say that you cannot go far wrong if you insist on the highest references!"

www.ingramcontent.com/pod-product-compliance
Ingram Content Group UK Ltd.
Pitfield, Milton Keynes, MK11 3LW, UK
UKHW041421180426
11947UKWH00007B/227